BAAC
6/2020

SENSATION

I shot an angry look at Paramount as I braced myself and started to rise from the floor. He put a hand up to his mouth, as if to hide his snickering after having knocked me down. I can't explain what happened next, but fury such as I had never felt - all-encompassing and all-controlling - exploded inside me.

I switched into super speed, moving so fast that later, even on film slowed down as much as possible, my movements were a blur. I grabbed the chair I had been sitting in, and in one smooth motion folded it up, spun around, and hit Paramount with it squarely on the chin in uppercut fashion.

I mentioned before that I don't actually have super strength, but when moving at top speed I can mimic it pretty well. Paramount's head snapped back and he went sailing bodily up into the air. He hit the back wall with an audible smack that shattered plaster, then slid down to the floor.

I stood frozen, still gripping the chair. I seriously doubted that I had hurt him; at only sixteen, Paramount was already practically invulnerable, like his father. The lick I'd just laid on him was probably akin to an adult getting poked in the eye by a baby. It catches you a little off-guard, but it's more irritating than painful, with no lasting effect.

Sadly, I was right. Paramount started to get up...

SENSATION

SENSATION
A Superhero Novel

By

Kevin Hardman

SENSATION

Cover Design by Isikol

This book is published by I&H Recherche Publishing.

ISBN: 978-1-937666-04-0

Printed in the U.S.A.

ACKNOWLEDGMENTS

I would like to thank the following for their help with this book: First and foremost, the good LORD, who has been generous in bestowing many blessings in my life; my brother Darrell, who made a career out of sharing his comic books with me; my children, who served as my inspiration; and my wife, who has always encouraged my writing, even when I myself thought I was better-suited for other things.

SENSATION

PROLOGUE

In a remote corner of a major metropolitan city, in a deserted industrial wasteland of gutted factories and boarded warehouses, deep underground and far from prying eyes, menacing figures gather to plot the fate of the world.

There are six of them, but not all have appeared in person. In fact, only one may be said to be physically present in the room. Three others appear by hologram, ghostly blue projections emanating from unknown origins. Another speaks through a robotic representative, its weaponry and offensive capabilities plainly evident. The last speaks through a golem - a human body without a mind of its own.

"Omen, why have you called this meeting?" The speaker is the golem, a female this time, its high voice oddly hollow but eerily suited to the empty look in its eyes. It sits at a marble top table next to the robot. "I thought we agreed there would be limited communication until all was in readiness."

"Yes, that was indeed the plan, Slate," Omen responds. He is a robed and hooded figure. He sports a neatly trimmed black beard, and might under ordinary circumstances be considered quite handsome but for one disturbing feature: his eyes – dark and brooding at even the best of times – are completely black, evidence that at the moment he is entertaining some vision of the future. "Unless there was an emergency."

"What manner of emergency?" asks one of the holograms, a swirling mass of disjointed shapes and

1

obscure images – the projection of the extra-dimensional alien known as Summit.

"A new variable has arisen, a deviation that cannot be accounted for and which might actually interfere with our plans."

"How is that possible?" asks Versus, another hologram. "You claim to be the most powerful precognitive on the planet, able to see the future in clear and unerring detail. We've staked everything on your purportedly infallible ability – and arrogant claims – that success was assured."

"Precognitive does not mean omniscient. There are always variables in play, other possibilities and probabilities that could take on the shape of reality."

"Now he tells us!"

"Calm yourself, Versus," says the golem. "Tell us, Omen, what is this variable? Whatever its nature, we will find a resolution. We've come too far to be denied now."

"It's not a what; it's a who."

"Then the solution is obvious." The robot's claws extend and etch deep grooves into the marble table as they retract. "We merely need a name."

"The one they call Kid Sensation."

SENSATION

Chapter 1

I was taken aback when I saw it. At the time, I was in my Mohawk persona: six feet six inches of impressive mocha-colored muscle and incomparable physique. (Not to mention the intimidating haircut, the source of my pseudonym.) I had just turned in another super criminal, Drillbit, and was waiting at the police station for confirmation that the reward on him had been transferred to my account. I just happened to glance at the wanted posters on the wall next to the on-duty desk, and that's when I saw it.

WANTED

INFORMATION LEADING TO THE WHEREABOUTS OF THE SUPER KNOWN AS KID SENSATION.

NAME: UNKNOWN

ALIASES: KID; THE KID; KID SENSATION

POWERS: FLIGHT; SHAPESHIFTING; SUPER SPEED; TELEPATHY; TELEKINESIS; TELEPORTATION; PHASING; BELIEVED TO HAVE OTHER POWERS BUT NATURE UNKNOWN.

SENSATION

DOB: UNKNOWN

DISTINGUISHING MARKS: UNKNOWN

LAST KNOWN
WHEREABOUTS: UNKNOWN

KNOWN ASSOCIATES: UNKNOWN

REWARD: $1,000,000

CONTACT THE ALPHA LEAGUE WITH ANY
PERTINENT INFORMATION

Underneath the word "WANTED" was a grainy photo, a frame frozen from the interview Kid Sensation had given to that reporter, Sylvia Gossett, two years earlier. It showed a young, dark-skinned teen from the neck up.

I tapped the poster and turned to the officer on duty. "Why is this here?"

The officer glanced at where I was pointing. "Ah…thinking about going after the Kid, huh? That would be a sweet payday."

"Except he's not a criminal."

"Are you kidding?" The officer was incredulous. "After what he did?"

I fumed silently, trying to keep the emotion out of my voice and face.

"This poster doesn't list a crime," I said flatly. "It doesn't even say that he's wanted for anything. It just says that they want info leading to his whereabouts."

The officer shrugged. "So?"

"So, his picture shouldn't be hanging up here with the scum of the universe - these freaks, fugitives, and felons who committed real crimes."

"Hey man," the officer held his hands up defensively, "we just post what the Watch Commander tells us."

I grunted my disapproval. A few more minutes passed by in uncomfortable silence. Then a computer in front of the officer beeped.

"Alright," the officer said, "the reward should be in your account."

I turned to leave, still upset about the wanted poster.

"You really should think about going after Kid Sensation, though," the officer said to my back. "Even without the reward, catching him would make you so famous you could write your own ticket."

I left the police station in a huff. Why would I want to capture Kid Sensation? I *am* Kid Sensation.

****

I stepped out of the police station into the sunny warmth of a beautiful summer day. I had a little time to kill, so I decided to take a nice leisurely walk, which is not something I do very often. On this particular occasion, though, it gave me a chance to be alone with my thoughts. Thus, it wasn't until after about fifteen minutes of random strolling that I realized, with a bit of a start, that I was being followed. Not a problem in and of itself (because I knew I could shake practically any pursuer without a lot of effort), but still somewhat annoying.

SENSATION

I was walking down a busy street in the shopping district at the time. Although my height as Mohawk made me stand out, the crowd was just dense enough that any tail I'd picked up could lose track of me for a second.

I hadn't really seen the person following me, just felt their heightened anxiety when I passed out of their line of sight for a moment. As an empath, I typically tune out the emotions of people in close proximity to me, much like the average person will disregard conversations going on around them. However, my follower's initial panic at momentarily losing track of me was the equivalent of having someone shout my name from across the street. In fact, I normally would have detected this level of distress from someone a lot sooner. Unfortunately, I was distracted by two things: the wanted poster I'd seen in the police station, and - more importantly - an odd buzzing sensation in my head, which usually indicated the manifestation of another power.

For a second, I wondered what power it was. It wasn't super strength; when I'd awakened with my head buzzing that had been the first thing I'd tested by trying to lift the sofa with one hand. No luck. Despite all my abilities (and hopeful prayers), that was one of the few super powers I didn't have. Or didn't have *yet*, since it appeared that - from the perspective of developing super powers – I was still in puberty to a certain extent.

Turning my thoughts back to my stalker, I stopped for a minute to look in the show window of a jewelry store. While pretending to admire a tennis bracelet, I reached out empathically and felt for him…there, behind me and to the left – nervousness, dread, and a number of other bundled-up emotions directed at me. I glanced casually in that direction, pinpointing the source of the feelings I was picking up. A small, pinched-faced man with a scraggly beard and sunglasses was looking in my direction. He was no one I knew.

For a brief moment, I considered confronting him. As Mohawk, I enjoyed a reputation as a fearsome bounty hunter. I had captured several notorious criminals – super criminals, to be precise – and was starting to garner particular attention in certain circles. Could this guy be the friend of someone I'd brought in? Was he looking for payback? Was he some kind of fan?

I looked at my watch. I was supposed to meet Braintrust shortly for the debrief; I didn't have a lot of time to mess around. Bearing that in mind, I could just disappear or zip away, but I decided to have a little fun. (Plus I was a little bit curious.)

Next to the jewelry store was a shop that sold vintage clothing. I ducked inside, grabbed a duffel bag, some sandals, a pair of jeans and a '60s Summer-of-Love t-shirt with a peace symbol on it, then headed to the changing rooms. One of the store clerks, a perky young blonde with a ring of thorns tattooed around one arm, made a move in my direction as if to assist me, but changed her mind after seeing the look on my face.

It took me all of thirty seconds to change out of my Mohawk clothes and into the new apparel. I hadn't checked the sizes of anything, but it didn't matter; I could make them fit (or rather, being a shapeshifter, make *myself* fit *them*). I stuffed my old clothes, including shoes, into the duffel bag and walked out of the changing room a skinny White kid. If the store clerk found it strange that the six-six hulking brute who went in had been replaced by a suburbanite teenager coming out, she gave no sign. I ripped the tags off everything and presented them to the girl behind the checkout counter.

"I'm just going to wear these out," I said, as she accepted the tags with a raised eyebrow. I glanced outside. Yep, Pinchface was out there, trying to appear nonchalant while conspicuously peeping through the store window.

I passed him on my way out after paying for my items. Again, I got a jumble of emotions coming off him in waves, but nothing really indicating menace. I decided not to worry about it. For his part, Pinchface never even looked at me, so focused was he on watching for Mohawk. I walked out the door and past him without meriting a glance.

I went around the corner and ducked down an alley. I checked to make sure no one was watching, then teleported back to my condo.

SENSATION

Chapter 2

The complex that housed my condo was one of the latest outposts of a twenty-year gentrification project. Cash-rich developers had spent the last two decades buying up dilapidated homes and public housing projects in the inner city. The typical pattern usually involved demolishing said domiciles, and then constructing uber-chic residences that young professionals would pay through the nose for. The desire to have the places where they lived close to their jobs (as well as the nearby bars, clubs, etc.) had led to a revitalization of the downtown area where most of the young people worked.

I popped into my condo in the master bedroom. Normally, I would have materialized a few blocks away as George Boring (the identity I used to buy the place) and walked into my building, which is a converted apartment complex. Even though, as a teleporter, I never have to bother with doors, I have to keep up appearances and being "normal" by letting the neighbors and staff see me once in a while. (I learned this the hard way when, a few months after buying the condo, the off-duty cop who works security at night asked me for some ID and proof of residence.)

The condo itself was a nice three-bedroom, two-bath unit furnished in a modern contemporary style. Looking around, I could see that the place could use a little dusting, although I really didn't care if it got done or not. The truth of the matter is that I really didn't live there. It was little more than a way station for me, a place I popped into occasionally to change clothes (or my appearance) so it didn't see a lot of regular use – especially during the school year.

SENSATION

Still, my grandfather had insisted that if I was going to be creeping around behind my mother's back acting out as Mohawk, then I needed to have a separate base of operations. Thus, the condo, which my grandfather actually loaned me the money for (and which I had since paid back with the bounties I'd earned).

It wasn't exactly a secret lair, but I had come to appreciate having a place that was solely mine, even if I didn't spend a whole lot of time there. But I guess that had been my grandfather's experience talking, and as with so many other things, he had been right.

Wasting no time, I tossed the duffel bag with Mohawk's clothes on the bed, catching a glimpse of myself in the dresser mirror. I was back to being me again – a tall, slender sixteen-year-old guy with short, dark curly hair and a natural complexion that looked something between fair and moderately tan. Thankfully, the recently-purchased clothes still fit. Obviously I had chosen a body type close to my own true state.

I checked my watch: five minutes until my meeting with Braintrust. I contemplated teleporting to our meeting place – one of Braintrust's safe houses – but it always seems rude to just pop up like that, even when people are expecting you. Flying there was a possibility, but flight – while not uncommon – is a rare enough ability that people flying under their own power get noticed, and BT would kill me if I inadvertently brought attention to one of his hideouts. That left me with the option of running.

Being a speedster is cool, but it does have a couple of drawbacks. First and foremost, it's hell on your clothes. The friction caused by someone zipping along at 1,000 miles per hour, arms whipping back and forth and legs rubbing together, will usually wear a hole in ordinary fabric in less time that it takes to tell about it. (Assuming it doesn't catch fire, which has actually happened to some speedsters on occasion). In short, you need specially designed clothes – or rather, clothes manufactured with special material.

Fortunately, I had a nice range of clothes that fit the bill. After super speed manifested as another one of my powers, my grandfather had called in a couple of favors (one of the benefits of having a former superhero in the family) and had some items made. They looked and felt just like regular clothes – you couldn't tell the difference between the jeans and t-shirt I decided to wear and normal apparel – but wouldn't go to pieces if you zipped across a couple of state lines in them.

Dressed, I teleported to a nearby park. I typically only ran at super speed from open spaces, having discovered early on that speeding from indoors tends to have certain disadvantages, like wearing a trail through your carpet in a hurry, leaving a whirlwind behind you, and more.

It was summer, but there were surprisingly few people in the park. I didn't worry about anybody seeing me pop in, as I wouldn't be there long enough for them to notice much about me. As I prepared to run, my vision telescoped, and faraway details came neatly into view. Super-vision is an ancillary power of super speed; it doesn't do you much good to be able to run at Mach 3 if you can't see something like a car coming until it's right on top of you. People assume that a lot of the old-time speedsters – like Zipp and The Bullet – retired because they were slowing down and had lost a step. Most of them, however, still had their speed when they hung up their capes. Their eyes had just gone bad.

I was meeting Braintrust at a sprawling but rundown estate about five miles outside of town – roughly fifteen miles away. I took off, calculating that I could get there in about two minutes without pushing it. As I ran, I either sidestepped or gently moved insects and various bits of debris out of my way. The movements of speedsters – when they run slow enough to be seen – often tend to appear kind of herky-jerky, with random hand movements. The truth of the matter is that, unless you wanted to arrive at your destination as bug-spattered as the windshield of a '57 Chevy on the highway, you had to either go around or move a lot of things.

I arrived at BT's hideout (a place I had mentally dubbed "The Compound") about five seconds ahead of schedule. It was about a ten-acre spread, with various buildings seemingly scattered at random across the property. The main building was a hundred-year-old mansion that, from the outside, looked like it would collapse if someone sneezed too hard around it. Waist-high weeds sprouted on both sides of the road that led up to the house.

I dropped out of super speed about a hundred yards from the front door. I was expected, but it seemed polite to give BT notice that I was on the grounds. I casually sauntered up to the door, which opened up before I even got close enough to knock.

A man stood in the doorway. He was slim, of average height, with dark hair. He sported a goatee, and wore a golf shirt and khaki pants. He was a Braintrust clone.

SENSATION

Braintrust, as I understood it, wasn't just a single person but rather a huge cluster of clones that shared a single hive mind, for lack of a better term. The clone at the door was the first that I'd met and the one that I had the most interaction with, so I mentally named him BT-1. Although I tended to think of Braintrust as a "he," some of the clones were actually female. Once, when I was younger, I had asked him about it. He had laughed at that, then explained to me that – up to a certain stage of their development in the womb – all babies were the same. However, with the right controls in place, you could manipulate the gender, among other things, whichever way you wanted.

Thus, I didn't really know if the original Braintrust was male or female. To be honest, I didn't really know whether he – it – was even human. Once, when he was helping me with my telepathy, I'd tried to secretly probe him and find out if he was a man or a woman. All I got was the impression of a massive intellect and an unquenchable thirst for knowledge. As to physical appearance, I could sense its existence, but not its shape or form. (Of course, telepathy isn't my forte, so I can be forgiven if I botched that particular operation.)

"You made it," said the clone, reaching out to shake my hand.

"Naturally," I replied as I shook his hand and then stepped by him into the house.

The inside was a complete contrast to the exterior. Whereas the outside looked like it was ready to fall down, the interior was well-kept and expensively maintained. I was in an enormous living room, which was decorated in an early twentieth-century style. Both walls had a winding staircase that crept up to what appeared to be an opulent second floor. The entire place was decked out in some expensive brand of marble that covered the floor from wall to wall. In short, it always reminded me of my great-grandmother's house, on the few occasions I had visited her when she had been alive. Everything in her home had looked old and expensive, and I had been afraid to touch anything.

BT (all of the Braintrust clones answer to "BT") started walking towards the kitchen, obviously expecting me to follow. "So, tell me how it went."

I fell into step just behind him. "About as expected. Your info was good, as always. He was right where you said he'd be."

I then prepared to launch into a rehash of the morning's events, how I (as Mohawk) had captured and claimed the bounty on another wanted fugitive with super powers. This time it had been Drillbit. He basically had hands that could punch through just about anything, although some things (like bank vaults) took longer than others.

"And the inhibitor collar worked fine?" BT asked, cutting me off before I even began to speak.

"If by fine you mean 'terribly' or 'like crap,' then yeah, it was great. You'll get a Nobel Prize for your work."

Inhibitor collars were, as the name implies, devices that inhibit or block supers from using their powers. The idea had been around for decades and various prototypes had even been developed. The problem was that inhibitor collars didn't come in a one-size-fits-all model. Each had to be specialized for a particular person. A collar meant to stop a speedster wouldn't have an effect on a mind reader. One meant to prevent a flyer might not work on someone with super-agility.

In essence, inhibitor collars had to be custom-made to block a specific individual from using his powers. However, few supers were going to let you use them as a guinea pig to design something meant to take away their powers. In fact, some were downright proactive about it – especially those who were part of the criminal element. The result was that people found to be, or thought to be, working on inhibitor projects had a nasty habit of disappearing. Forever.

BT's inhibitors worked maybe twenty-five percent of the time. In an ideal world, once I knew where a criminal was, I should have only had to (a) wait for an opportunity to teleport next to him as Mohawk, and then (b) put the inhibitor around his neck before he knew what was happening, thereby taking away any special abilities he had. In actuality, what usually happened was that the criminal retained his full powers, then came at Mohawk with murder in his eyes.

That's when we'd usually go to Plan B, which typically involved me teleporting the fugitive to a nullifier cage. A nullifier is different than an inhibitor. It's a field generated through the use of quantum mechanics. It's not really something I fully understand, but it causes some kind of temporal shift, so that someone with super abilities is unable to access their powers. But nullifiers were expensive and not really practical, although they had their uses (primarily in special jail cells and prisons).

Our nullifier cage was essentially a cell in an abandoned warehouse. After teleporting someone into it, the room would fill with knockout gas, and then Mohawk would haul them, unconscious, into the nearest police station for the reward. That was essentially what had happened with Drillbit.

BT groaned at my comments, as I gave him a ten-second spiel of the capture and returned his inhibitor to him. It was basically a circular metal band about three inches in length and half an inch thick, with a number of colored diodes that flashed when it was in operation. To be frank, it bore something of a resemblance to an ancient Egyptian necklace.

Braintrust and I were partners to a certain extent. He located wanted super criminals, and I would bring them in and collect the reward. However, we never split the money. Knowledge was the coin of the realm where BT was concerned. Although the inhibitor hadn't taken away Drillbit's powers, it had scanned him and taken biometric readings, which BT would use to further refine the device. That was his payment.

BT walked through a swinging door and into the kitchen. Without breaking stride, I phased – becoming insubstantial – and literally passed through the door like a ghost, then re-solidified on the other side. A huge granite-top island stood in the center of the kitchen, covered with grilled steaks, hot dogs, hamburgers, donuts, cheesecake, and a number of other delectable treats. This spread was meant for me, so I pulled up a nearby stool and started eating, beginning with a juicy steak.

Running at super speed switches my metabolism into high gear. The result was that I needed to replace the calories I'd burned, and – per our usual routine – BT always had a buffet laid out for me. Nearby, a cook stood working over a six-burner gas stove, with all of the burners covered. The cook was another BT clone; this one had four arms.

SENSATION

BT's clones tended to be specialized. In other words, they were designed to perform a distinct function, and therefore tended to have the necessary characteristics to do their jobs. Thus, the cook had twice the usual number of arms. For the millionth time I wondered how BT formed these clones – whether there was some unique biological process that let him grow them off his own physical body (whatever that was), or if he created them through some artificial means in a lab.

BT took a seat while I ate. "I really thought the inhibitor would work this time."

"Not a big deal," I shrugged, talking around a mouth full of food. "No harm, no foul."

"Well, I'll need some time to find the next target, as well as tweak the inhibitor and reset the nullifier."

I simply nodded, shoving a piece of cheesecake into my mouth. Because of the nullifier, I usually had about a two-month break in-between going after fugitives. Standard nullifiers give off a particular energy signature when in use. Because that signature can be traced, BT designed a nullifier that operates on a slightly different principal. I didn't really understand it, but the end result was that - although it doesn't give off an energy signature - our nullifier had to be "reset" after each use, which usually took about sixty days.

There were actually a lot of non-powered criminals out there I could have gotten the reward for whenever the nullifier was out of commission, but there were normal bounty hunters who could take them down. There was no need for me to take food out of the mouth of another working stiff. (Not to mention the fact that I was still in high school and – at least during the school year – had class during the day.)

"So," BT continued, "other than the occasional capture of wanted felons, how's the rest of your summer been?"

I held out my hand and wobbled it side-to-side. "So-so."

Speaking frankly, summer vacation wasn't anything that got me particularly excited the way it did most kids. I didn't have a lot of friends. My summers were normally spent hanging out with my grandfather, which usually meant training. Not that I was complaining.

"Well," he continued, "don't forget that there's a game tomorrow."

I frowned. I knew where this was headed. "Yeah, I'm still thinking about it."

"And don't forget that there are tryouts in about two weeks."

This is where I knew he'd been going with the conversation, and I didn't want to think about it.

Every year, kids from ages fourteen to eighteen could, if they had a super power, try out to join one of the superhero teams. If you were good enough, or had enough potential, you'd get recruited to go study in-residence at the Academy (where they help develop your powers) with one of the superhero teams as your sponsor. If you succeeded there, the expectation was that you'd eventually get an offer to join the team that had supported you. In a sense, it was a lot like being a high school athlete who college scouts were trying to recruit.

My tryout two years earlier had been a disaster of epic proportions. (It was also what had landed me my own "Wanted" poster.) It was something that I tried, unsuccessfully, to put out of my mind almost every day of the week. Being reminded of it now didn't help.

"It's time you put the past behind you," he went on.

"Yeah, right. Because my tryout last time was such a rousing success."

"You know, when you think about it, you didn't really do anything wrong. And you can't tell me that you haven't been giving it some thought."

"Well, I haven't," I lied. "I've had other things on my mind – like who's been following me."

BT was a little startled. "What?"

"Yeah, someone was following me today. Some guy I haven't seen before."

"When? Where?"

"In the shopping district today, after I brought in Drillbit."

I launched into a quick explanation of how I'd sensed Pinchface and then given him the slip.

BT frowned in thought for a moment before asking a question.

"Can you show me what he looked like?"

"Sure."

I closed my eyes in concentration. My intent was to plant an image of Pinchface in BT's mind. Normally, I don't go mucking about in other people's brains. As I already mentioned, the telepathic stuff really isn't in my wheelhouse. In fact, reading minds was, for me, like taking a bath in someone else's vomit. (From my standpoint, people had a lot of mental "filth" in their brains.) It usually made me nauseous - my grandfather once compared it to a doctor who gets squeamish at the sight of blood - so in my opinion, it's not a talent that I truly possess, despite technically being a telepath.

SENSATION

Reading BT was different, though. His mind was the exact opposite of other people's: clean, sterile — antiseptic, in fact.

BT opened his mind to me, so I had no trouble getting inside. As I said, though, he had a titanic intellect, and I knew that he could shut most telepaths out if he wanted to. Right now, however, his mind was a clear, open space, a dimensional void where nothing existed but bright, pervasive light.

I focused on the picture I had of Pinchface in my head. The light in BT's mind shimmered, started taking on color and form. It was an oval at first, an upside-down egg that began assuming features I recognized: cheeks, eyes, a nose.... Suddenly, the face solidified in all its detail. I withdrew from his brain.

"Got it," BT said. "I'll check it out and let you know."

As I said, BT trucked in the area of information. He'd have no trouble finding out who Pinchface was.

"You also said that you didn't notice him initially because you were distracted," he continued. "A new power?"

"Yeah - good guess - but I don't know what it is yet."

"But you have the sensation that usually accompanies a new ability?"

"Yeah."

"Hmmm...maybe it's an augmentation of your existing powers rather than something new. Care to run through some exercises?"

I shrugged. "Sure thing. I'm in no rush."

We then went through a quick series of exercises that involved me using each of my powers. We started with invisibility. As usual, when I turned invisible, my vision automatically switched over to the infrared spectrum. It was another ancillary power; once my eyes became invisible, I couldn't see across the visible light spectrum the way normal people do, so I used infrared (although, in truth, I could also see across other wavelengths of light).

After invisibility, we went through all of my other primary and secondary powers as well: flight, teleportation, phasing, and so on – the whole shebang. It took a little bit of time because, to be frank, I've got way more powers than the average super.

"I'm not seeing anything outside the ordinary – for you, that is," BT stated, shaking his head when we'd finished. "In all honesty, though, I still don't fully understand your power set."

"What's to understand? I've got super powers, just like a lot of other people."

"It's not quite as banal as you make it sound. There are roughly seven billion people on this planet. Approximately two million of them are supers, or metas, or whatever term you like for someone with super powers. Ninety-nine percent of those have powers that barely register as anything above normal, like being able to float half an inch off the ground. That remaining one percent consists of those individuals who have powers that fall into Levels A through D, the ones that generally come to mind when we think of supers."

"And A-Level - as the highest-ranked - would be along the lines of the Alpha League, I take it?"

BT nodded. The Alpha League was the premiere superhero team on the planet. Led by the invincible

Alpha Prime, they were the best of the best, the superheroes all others were measured against.

"But," he continued, "even among groups like the Alpha League, you'll usually find that most people only have one or two primary powers – nothing like the smorgasbord you've got."

"Well, you just said it yourself: some people are born with no powers whatsoever. It only stands to reason that someone would be born at the other end of the spectrum with lots of abilities. I guess I just got lucky and hit the jackpot."

"Yes, but a lot of your powers are completely redundant. For instance, you don't need super speed *and* teleportation; one is almost just as good as the other. You don't need shapeshifting *and* the ability to turn invisible; both are camouflage techniques, but why have two of them? Likewise, I'm not sure that you need to be both a telepath *and* an empath – knowing what people are thinking as well as what they're feeling – although those two often go hand-in-hand."

"So basically, when they were giving out powers, I had a special two-for-one coupon in my pocket."

"I guess that's one way to look at it. Except your powers keep expanding – even though you already have almost all of the highly-regarded abilities."

"Except super strength," I reminded him.

"Yes," he acquiesced with a slight nod, "but you can mimic it well enough that you don't need it."

I knew what he meant. Basically, when I'm moving at super speed, much of what I can do is amplified and can give the impression of having super strength. As an experiment, BT had once had me hit a baseball at normal speed. I got off a good hit, but nothing to write home about. He had then had me hit a second ball at super speed; it landed almost a mile away.

Still, being able to mimic super strength and actually having it were two different things. Personally, I preferred to have the real McCoy, and I stated as much.

"Talk about ingratitude," BT said, shaking his head in mock disappointment. "Most people would give their right arm for just one of your powers, and all you can do is cry about what you can't do."

"Fine, I'm a big baby. So if that's it, I'm going to go home and cry myself to sleep."

"Yeah, that's it. Give your mother and grandfather my regards."

Chapter 3

After finishing with Braintrust, I teleported home. My real home. Although the apartment was effectively my secret lair, I actually lived with my mother in a quaint little two-story in the suburbs. I appeared upstairs in my bedroom, and almost immediately found myself under psychic attack.

A good telepath is like a professional safecracker. They can stealthily sneak into your mind, deftly spinning the tumblers of your psyche until they find a way in. Then they take whatever valuables they can find and leave without you ever being aware of it.

Of course, some telepaths don't care about being nimble. Rather than adroitly picking the locks of your brain, they come at you like a SWAT team on a raid, using a battering ram on the door of your mind and rushing in to suppress any resistance and take control of the premises. This attack was of the second kind.

Thinking of the mind as a house is a pretty good way to conceptualize it, although a better analogy is probably a castle with a lot of nooks and crannies. Just like a real castle, you need to fortify your defenses; it doesn't hurt to give yourself a mental moat, high walls, etc.

My attacker came at me like a blunt instrument. It was an attack on all fronts at once. However, there was no strategy involved; it was merely an attempt to overwhelm me with sheer force of will. In short, my mind-castle was under siege on all sides.

I fought back valiantly, mentally firing arrows and dumping hot tar on my attacker. He didn't give up, though. What he lacked in strategy, he made up for in strength, and it wasn't long before he found a crack in my walls. He worried at it, expanded it, and soon he had an army pouring through. Which is exactly what I wanted.

My nemesis soon came to realize that his makeshift entry into my castle was a dead end; it led nowhere. But before he could get back out, the exit sealed up behind him. Then the walls started closing in. He hammered at them without avail, gave a mental screech, then evaporated from my mind.

<Nice try, old man,> I thought. Less than a minute had passed since I had popped into my room, but I was sweating and breathing hard. Mental battles can take a lot out of you.

<Not bad,> came the reply, with a mental chuckle. <But there's always room for improvement. Your reaction time was slow, and your defense was cumbersome. Plus it took me way too long to fall into your trap. You could have sprung it a lot sooner. That's the thing about psychic attacks: they have to invade *your* mind, come onto *your* turf. Remember: your mind, your rules. Come by when you get a moment; I want to talk to you about something.>

With that, contact broke off. I beamed; it may have sounded like he had some complaints, but that was high praise coming from the old man, my grandfather. I vaulted down the stairs two at a time and headed to the kitchen for a drink.

"Jim?" It was my mother. As usual, she was in her office. Mom was a moderately successful author of superhero romances (albeit under a pseudonym), so she tried to spend at least four hours per day writing.

"It's me," I answered. "Just getting a drink of water."

SENSATION

"Have you eaten yet?" I heard the slight squeak of her chair as she rose, and the firm cadence of her footsteps as she headed towards the kitchen. "Do you want me to make you something?"

"No, I'm fine," I stated as she came into view.

In typical mom fashion, she came over and began picking at my clothes, removing inconsequential strands of hair, lint and the like.

"So, any big plans for tonight? It's Friday, you know."

"Not really," I replied. "Probably just stay here and play video games."

"You've only got a few weeks before school starts again. Don't you want to go hang out with your friends?"

"Mom, I don't have any friends. You know that."

"Acquaintances then. People you know. People your own age."

I was exasperated. It wasn't the first time I'd heard this.

"Mom, I'm fine. We both know I'm not like other kids. Normal kids."

"All the more reason for you to be around them. Or at least other people who could be considered your peers."

"Fine. I know where you're going with this. If it'll make you happy, I'll go to the stupid football game tomorrow."

Suddenly she was glowing. "Cool!"

"Mom, only geriatrics say 'cool' any more. Or shut-ins who haven't kept up with the times."

"Well, this geriatric shut-in has a date tonight."

I stood in stunned silence and just looked at her. Mom was about five-ten, with straight, dark hair that dropped a little below her shoulders. She had a complexion that was slightly darker than mine, and huge almond-shaped eyes that gave her a striking appearance. It had come as a great shock to me years earlier when I found out that most people considered my mother to be exotically beautiful. (And it didn't hurt that she looked a lot younger than her actual age.)

"Hey!" My mother snapped her fingers. "Say something."

"Uh...have a good time?"

"Don't you even want to know who it's with?"

Her eyes, which normally appeared blue, flashed purple, indicating mock anger. This was one of the two physical indications of her odd genetic inheritance. The other was her pointed, elfin ears, which gave her an even more exotic appearance when seen. Outside the house she wore contacts to hide her eyes, and she always kept her hair over her ears.

I shrugged. "No, you're old enough to make your own decisions. I trust your judgment."

She gave me a mock punch on the arm, then a hug before going back to her office. I grabbed a bottle of water from the refrigerator and headed out the back door. I twisted off the cap and took a swig as I walked towards the apartment where my grandfather lived above our garage.

Technically, it was his house that we lived in. Mom and I had been on our own before moving here eleven years earlier, living on the other side of the country. My father had been out of the picture since before I was born (plus we never really talked about him), so my grandfather was the only family and support system we had.

SENSATION

Even though the house actually had four bedrooms, Gramps had decided that he needed his own space and moved into the garage apartment, giving us the main house. As I walked up the stairs to the entrance, his voice rang out in my mind.

<Come on in. Door's open.>

I opened the door and stepped inside Wonderland.

Frankly speaking, I loved coming to my grandfather's apartment. Gramps was a telepath – at one time the most powerful on the planet, possibly the most powerful who ever lived. Known as Nightmare, he could invade the mind of any villain, know their plans, make them see their worst nightmare (hence the name), take control of their minds, etc. He could incapacitate with a thought, changing the course of any battle in seconds.

His apartment was full of mementos and keepsakes from his time as an active superhero. The mask of a famed supervillain, the deactivated weapon from another, photos of him with famous people. Coming to his apartment was, for me, like going to an amusement park. Plus, I had grown up on his stories, which had made me dream of one day being a superhero – until the train wreck of my tryout.

Gramps was sitting on the sofa, watching television and eating cookies. Despite being in his sixties, he had the frame and appearance of someone twenty years younger. His dusky skin had few wrinkles, although his hair had begun taking on a salt-and-pepper hue a few years before.

I took a cookie and sat down next to him on the sofa. He was watching the rebroadcast of a football game from years earlier. In fact, it appeared to be a Super

Bowl, but I couldn't recall from which year. I was chomping at the bit to tell him what happened with Drillbit and he knew it, but we sat there watching the game in silence for a few minutes until they broke away for a commercial.

"Alright," he said, turning to me. "Spill it."

I could have just said that I popped Drillbit into a nullifier cell and gassed him, but I'd learned from my grandfather the art of being a good storyteller – especially where supervillains were concerned. Thus, I did a reverse CliffsNotes and dragged a ten-second anecdote out into a full-length novel. By the time I finished, he was grinning.

"Not bad," he noted, "but Drillbit's not what I would consider a real challenge."

He didn't elaborate further, but he didn't have to. Super powers don't equate to a super brain, and Drillbit wasn't the brightest bulb in the socket. Gramps looked lost in thought for a moment, probably reflecting back on one of his old battles. Whatever story it was, I'd probably heard it a hundred times before, but I was ready to hear it again if he wanted to tell it. (As I said, he was a great storyteller.)

I glanced over at the mantel where my grandfather kept several of his most treasured keepsakes: pictures of the alien princess Indigo. My grandmother.

One of the photos was of them having a picnic. I looked at the photo, seeing the source of my mother's exquisite features: the elfin ears, the exotic eyes. My grandmother's white, porcelain-like skin stood in stark contrast to my grandfather's dark complexion.

Their marriage had been a great scandal at the time. Even though Indigo technically wasn't even human, she bore enough resemblance to a White female that the mere thought of a relationship between them had been enough to elicit protests. Violent reactions and hate mail had followed the announcement of their pending nuptials.

Nevertheless, they had persevered, and the union had even produced a child, my mother (although, as I understand, they had needed a little help from science, as their DNA had not been fully compatible). They had been happy, and would probably still be together had not an emergency on her homeworld called Indigo away. She had left and never returned, leaving my grandfather with an infant daughter to raise on his own.

Also on the mantel was a picture of me as a five-year-old. If you looked closely you could almost see the streaks of tears on my face. I hadn't wanted to take the picture then, but Gramps had told me it was important and I'd want a picture to remember that day, and he was right. It was the day I first developed my powers.

It was before we moved into my grandfather's house. My mother and I were living in a small, one-bedroom efficiency in an inexpensive but well-kept apartment complex. It would have been a very nice time in my life if not for a hulking brute of a bully named Bobby Trione.

Bobby was only nine, but of course he was much bigger than me, a five-year-old. He ruled the small playground at the apartment complex with an iron fist. In particular, there was a treehouse that Bobby had claimed as his own personal residence. In fact, there was a sign taped to the outside of it that said "Trione's Treehouse," and he took great offense at other children playing there without his permission.

SENSATION

Whenever Bobby wasn't around, I'd sneak into the treehouse and play inside anyway. However, one day I made the mistake of leaving one of my action figures there. It was a fatal error.

Bobby and I attended the same school, and one day shortly thereafter he cornered me and confronted me about playing in the treehouse. He had my action figure as proof, and when I was too slow in denying it, he started punching me. He punched hard and fast, screaming at me all the while to stay out of his treehouse, and before long I was bawling and doing little more than trying to curl up to avoid the worst of his blows.

As he hit me, I felt an odd pressure building in my brain. It was like a balloon, slowly filling with air, getting blown bigger and bigger. Then it popped.

Suddenly, there was no more shouting. No more punches. No more Bobby. In short, Bobby had disappeared, literally, and I was crying worse than I was when he was wailing on me. I knew Bobby was gone, and I knew that it was because of something I'd done - something terrible - but I didn't know what. I ran off wildly, heedless of where I was going, just wanting to get away. I eventually found my way to a corner of the school basement and hid there, crying for what seemed like forever.

A short time later, I heard voices and looked up to find my grandfather there. He was in town visiting – babysitting me, actually – while my mother attended a writer's camp. He'd kept a telepathic tab on me in those days and, having felt my mental distress, had come to find me. I tried explaining things, but couldn't quite get the words out. My grandfather shushed me, then slowly, gently, carefully peeked into my mind, pulling back

31

thoughts and memories like onion layers, to see what had happened. After a few minutes, he chuckled and told me everything would be fine.

It turns out that I had developed my first power – teleportation – and sent Bobby back to his treehouse. Early on, however, I wasn't very good at teleporting people, and if I did it the person had a tendency to arrive at their destination a little disoriented. That's what happened to Bobby. I popped him into the treehouse, but he couldn't get his bearings; he fell out and broke his arm. (And it couldn't have happened to a nicer guy.)

My grandfather took the picture of me that day. After my mother returned from her workshop, he had a very pointed talk with her, and three days later we moved across the country and into my grandfather's house. Shortly thereafter, he introduced me to BT, and they began training me to use my powers, among other things.

Reflecting on my memories of that day, I stayed chatting with my grandfather for about another hour, then left. As with my mother, I promised him that I would go to the football game. (Apparently that was what he'd wanted to talk to me about.)

I came back home and had a couple of sandwiches for dinner. Then I took a shower, watched a little television, and went to bed, hoping that a good night's rest would prepare me for Saturday's football game.

INTERLUDE

The Six Masters were gathered in their lair again, once more discussing their plans and how best to achieve their ends.

"I would give stronger endorsement to this plan," said Slate through his golem, this time a male, "if the destruction of the Alpha League was assured."

Apex, another cohort appearing by hologram, snorted. "Destroying the Alpha League is far easier said than done, and would consume far more resources than currently at our disposal. Trust me, I know. We need only restrict their ability to interfere, and those plans are already in motion."

"And what of the other problem – Kid Sensation? Where are we on that issue?"

"We are steadily closing in on him," Omen responded. "We'll have him at our mercy before long, and be in a position to nullify any effect he might have on our plans."

SENSATION

Chapter 4

The "football game" was actually more of a get-together that took place every weekend during the summer. It was sponsored by several of the superhero teams and was held at the Academy. In essence, it was a mix-and-mingle for kids with super powers. (Somewhere along the way, someone had figured out that a good way to help kids deal with the angst, anxiety, and isolation of growing up with super powers was to put them around peers.)

Attendance, however, was by invitation only, but BT had somehow arranged for me to be invited regularly. Basically, bright and early on Saturday mornings, you would appear at a designated place at a designated time. At that point, a car with tinted windows would take you to an airfield in the middle of nowhere, at which juncture you'd board a plane to take you to the Academy.

Once at the Academy, you could participate in a wide range of activities, including making use of the students' break room since most of them were home for summer vacation. But – at least for guys – the big draw was football. Having super powers often meant that you couldn't participate in sports against normal people. Thus, a lot of guys, especially those with super strength, really basked in opportunities like this to cut loose.

On this particular Saturday, I flew out with a group of about a dozen kids, ages ten to eighteen. Not a lot of people, but I knew that numerous planes from other cities would also be flying in teens. After we arrived, everyone would be able to break away to pursue their own interests. I didn't always play, but today I decided to get into the football game.

SENSATION

Truth be told, there wasn't one football game that took place but several. Teams would be put together and pitted against each other based on the abilities of the players. I always came to the game with minimal shapeshifting changes. There were only a few alterations to my face - higher cheeks, wider nose - to give me a slightly different appearance, while my body stayed essentially the same. Moreover, I hadn't displayed any notable super powers, so I was teamed with a group of people with moderate abilities and slotted against a team of similar talents in a game slated to start around noon.

Thankfully, you don't need super powers to enjoy football, and we had a blast. I got along really well with my teammates, which included a psychic named Claire Voyant; Smokescreen, who could blanket an area with dense fog; and Bounce, who could stretch his rubberized body to impressive lengths.

We were playing a pretty close contest that had seen several lead changes take place. We were down by four points with two minutes left in the game when we got the ball back for what was presumably the last time. Then Paramount and his gorilla squad showed up.

Everyone knew who Paramount was. He was the spoiled rich kid of super teens. As the son of Alpha Prime (who was universally acknowledged as the most powerful superhero in existence), he had an impeccable pedigree and he knew it. Still, because of who his father was, Paramount also had a lot to live up to. Moreover, he had grown up in the limelight, with those enormous expectations always perched on his shoulders. Most other people would have buckled under the pressure, but Paramount seemed to thrive on it. Not only had he been blessed with his father's statuesque physique and movie-star good looks, he had also inherited the most enviable of his powers: super strength, invulnerability, super speed.... About the only thing he lacked was flight, although - since he was only eighteen - there was still the possibility that his power set had not fully emerged. Still, even without the ability to fly, it was widely assumed that he would one day take his father's place as the gold standard for superheroes.

Like a lot of other wealthy brats, Paramount attracted sycophants like cow patties drew flies. He could usually be found with an entourage following him around and hanging on his every word. And almost all of them were guys with super strength. Those who can't lift a locomotive need not apply.

It was no different today, as Paramount sauntered out onto the field during our game, followed by a bunch of muscled brutes who I assumed were his teammates. "You guys need to wrap up. We're on next, and we need to get in a few minutes of practice before our game."

"We'll be finished in a minute," I said, barely paying attention to him.

"You don't understand," he continued. "You need to wrap up *now*."

"No, we're going to finish this game." I turned to Icarus, our quarterback, a cherubic guy with wings. "Call for the ball. The rest of you guys, get on the line."

My teammates slowly moved into position. Icarus looked hopefully over to the bleachers. There was always a superhero on duty to make sure the games didn't get out of hand. Today it was Esper. As her name implied, Esper was psychic, and she currently wore the crown of reigning telepath on the planet. She had barely been paying attention to the game before, but now she leaned forward, keenly interested, although she didn't interfere. Icarus looked nervously back and forth between me and Paramount.

"I'm out of here," he finally said, and zoomed up into the sky.

I cast a glance at Paramount, who had a self-satisfied grin on his face.

"Fine," I said, moving under center, "I'll be quarterback."

Suddenly, the captain of the opposing team interjected. "Hey, it's okay. We'll finish another time."

"No," I stated flatly. "My team is down by four points, and we're going to win this game."

"Then we'll forfeit," said the other captain diplomatically. "Right, guys?" His teammates nodded solemnly, and they collectively began walking to the sideline.

Paramount turned to me, totally smug, with his arms crossed.

"Opponents or not, we're finishing this game," I declared. When my teammates didn't seem to hear me, I shouted. "Smokescreen! Bounce! Get your butts on the line! The rest of you, too!"

My teammates looked a little unsure. Finally, Smokescreen shrugged and then got in place on the line of scrimmage. After a few seconds, everyone else followed suit.

Without warning, Paramount took a place on the other side of the line of scrimmage.

"No freebies today," he announced, getting into a three-point stance. "We're subbing for the defense." With vicious grins, the rest of his squad also got into position.

SENSATION

Several of my teammates exchanged nervous glances. Simply defying Paramount was one thing. Playing against him in a rough-and-tumble sport was something else entirely.

I didn't give them time to change their minds. I called for the ball, but I barely had it in my hands before Paramount was on me, sacking me - hard - for a loss. He was so fast that he almost got to me before the ball. He got up laughing as I took a moment to catch my breath before rising. I looked around and saw that the rest of our players had been equally roughhoused by his teammates - faces shoved forcefully into the turf, clothes covered in dirt. Paramount and his crew were playing us a lot tougher than what was called for - and thoroughly enjoying it.

The next two plays were essentially repeats of the first, ending up with me on my back and us taking a loss on the play. My teammates, likewise, were ferociously manhandled. I got up after third down feeling completely frustrated. I glanced at the scoreboard – only time for one more play. Nearby I saw Esper in the bleachers, still watching us intently. Suddenly I had an idea.

I opened up a tiny hole in my mental defenses and shot a thought to Claire Voyant.

<Claire, can you telepathically link us?>

<Who, us? Me and you?>

I ignored the undercurrent of schoolgirl giddiness in her mental tone. <No – the team. Can you link us telepathically?>

<Ah, sure. I mean I think so.>

A few seconds later we were all mentally linked, and I quickly explained my plan. There was no guarantee that it would work, but it was the last play of the game, so why not?

Everyone got in position. I looked to see if they were all ready and was happy to see gritty determination on a few faces. I began my snap count. Just before the ball was to be snapped, the area filled with dense fog in every direction for twenty yards. (Excellent job, Smokescreen.)

I heard Paramount's voice register surprise. "What the...?"

With normal vision I couldn't see anything, so – after breaking my telepathic link with the team – I switched over from the visible light spectrum to infrared and called for the ball. I caught it with ease.

Looking around, I could see almost everyone on the field (or rather, the energy they emitted). I saw Paramount rushing towards me, a huge swirling mass of crimson. From what I knew of his powers, I was sure he couldn't see me or the ball; he'd just headed in the last direction he'd seen me. I stepped nimbly to the side as he went rushing past.

Turning my attention downfield, I could see Bounce running all out, elongated neck and arms rising above the fog. I flung the ball down the field. His arms being stretched as far as they were, it was impossible to overthrow him. He caught the ball with ease and kept running without breaking stride. We were going to win!

I was so excited that I almost missed the huge scarlet body closing in on Bounce. It was Goon, a beastly member of Paramount's team. He wasn't what you would have called superfast, but he still had impressive speed. He closed the gap between him and Bounce in a frighteningly short span of time.

SENSATION

Goon dove at Bounce, catching him around the ankles. His momentum carried them forward, and – with great presence of mind – Bounce twisted in Goon's grip, his rubberized bones allowing him to turn his body backwards from the knees and above while his feet still faced forward. I recognized this as an effort on Bounce's part to buy a few precious microseconds by keeping his knees off the ground, and I loved him for it.

As his body arced towards the ground, Bounce extended his hand with the ball behind him towards the end zone. It was clearly going to be a photo finish, but just bare moments before his body hit the turf the ball crossed the plane of the goal line. I switched back to normal vision and opened my mind back up to Claire's team link.

<We won! We won! We won!> Bounce was mentally screaming.

My teammates all ran shouting towards the end zone, where Bounce still lay on the ground, holding the football like it was a million dollars. We lifted him up on our shoulders, still shouting. Even on the sideline, people were whooping and cheering. We were just starting to carry Bounce off the field when suddenly Paramount was there in front of us.

The cheers died down as he just stood there, glaring at us and breathing heavily. We lowered Bounce gently to the ground and walked off the field, feeling his murderous stare on our backs. As we reached the sideline, Bounce suddenly turned to me and tossed me the football, which he was still holding, and then tilted his head in Paramount's direction. I nodded and turned.

"Hey!" I shouted to get Paramount's attention. "For your game."

SENSATION

I tossed the ball to him in a lazy arc. A hazy blue glow filled Paramount's eyes. At the zenith of its approach, the football was obliterated as a beam of light from those eyes lanced out and touched it. A deafening silence suddenly settled on the entire assemblage, as everyone – including me – stood stunned.

Alpha Prime had an impressive and enviable power set: flight, super strength, super speed, and a myriad of others. However, the most impressive and deadly weapon in his arsenal was his Bolt Blast – powerful beams of energy that originated from his eyes and which would disintegrate anything they came into contact with: flesh, wood, steel, stone.... However, even against hardened criminals, AP would only use his Bolt Blast in the most dire situations.

Paramount had seemingly inherited this deadly power, but was less discriminating than his father in its use (as evidenced by Exhibit A, the football).

A bullhorn suddenly sounded in our minds, drowning out all other thoughts.

<PARAMOUNT!!! INSIDE! NOW!!!>

It was Esper, finally taking control of the situation.

<The rest of you, back to what you were doing!>

Paramount began walking sheepishly back towards the main campus.

I was preparing to go off with the rest of my teammates when I heard a follow-up command.

<Not you. Inside as well.>

Oh, great. What did I do?

SENSATION

Chapter 5

The Academy was actually a fascinating facility. First of all, as I understood it, the school actually existed in another dimension; the planes bringing the kids here every weekend actually had to fly through a dimensional vortex. That way, students enrolled there could be trained in relative peace and safety, far from prying eyes.

The area that made up the campus was huge, about as large as a mid-sized city, and had parks, forests, lakes, and more. (I suppose if you're going to create an extra-dimensional school for super-powered teens, there's no need to think small.) And students attending the Academy had every modern convenience you could think of, from food dispensers to holographic training rooms.

Up on the main campus, I'd been sitting in a chair outside the principal's office for about an hour. Actually, it was a chair outside the teacher's lounge, but it felt like waiting outside the principal's office. I wasn't sure why I was here; going over everything in my mind, I couldn't see why they'd need to talk to me. It was Paramount who had gone over the top out there on the field.

Without warning, I heard the knob turn and the door was opened by an Alpha League member called Mouse. He had joined the League about two years earlier, but was still pretty much a mystery. Contrary to what his name implied, he was a big guy - about six-three - and while clearly not a bodybuilder, he was obviously in great shape. He wasn't a household name by any stretch of the imagination and no one knew exactly what his powers were, but you don't get asked to join the Alpha League unless you're a big gun.

SENSATION

Mouse motioned me inside. I got up slowly, still concerned about what was happening here.

There were two other supers inside when I entered: Vixen, the empathic Siren, and Feral, an eight-foot hirsute monstrosity of muscle. Vixen and Mouse wore the trademark black-and-gold uniform of the Alpha League. As hairy as he was, Feral could have gotten away with wearing nothing at all. However, he had deigned to wear his uniform pants, although his torso was bare.

Mouse motioned to a chair and I sat. The three supers stood in a sort of semicircle around me. They were a few feet away, but it still felt like they were looming. Mouse glanced at some papers he was holding, then spoke.

"It says here that you go by Jim," he said. "Is it okay to call you that?"

I shrugged. "Fine by me."

"There's no indication of what your powers are," he went on.

"Apparently I have a talent for getting into trouble." This got a few chuckles and caused Vixen to chime in.

"You're not in trouble, sweetie," she said, leaning forward to pat my leg. Her voice was like honey, and where she touched my leg I felt a glowing warmth. Of course! She was a Siren! She had the power to sway the opposite sex to do whatever she wanted, among other things. I was suddenly on my guard.

"Then why does this feel like an interrogation?" I asked.

The three exchanged glances, and then Mouse pulled up a chair and sat down. Vixen and Feral did the same.

43

"We saw what happened out there." Feral this time. "We just want to talk to you about it."

"Wait a minute." I was confused. "You saw it?"

"Through Esper's eyes," Mouse explained. "She linked with us telepathically and shared her memories."

"Then if you saw everything and know what happened, why am I here?"

There was silence for a few seconds, and then Mouse spoke to his companions. "Guys, give us a few minutes."

Feral and Vixen rose and began walking out. As she left, Vixen leaned down and whispered something to Mouse, then tilted her head in my direction. Mouse shook his head vigorously in the negative. I had a sneaking suspicion she had just been told not to use her powers on me.

After they were gone, Mouse sighed. "You know where you are, right? The Academy." He swept his arm around in a wide, encompassing gesture. "The place where fledgling superheroes come to train. We have all kinds of kids here, with all kinds of powers. But sometimes that's not enough."

"What do you mean?" I asked.

"There are some things that you can't teach. There are some things you can't make up for, no matter what kind of power you have."

I didn't know where he was going with this. "Like what?"

"Like leadership." He leaned in close. "Look, I saw what you did with your team out there on the field. You took a ragtag bunch of kids with low power levels and got them to beat a team, that – on paper – was bigger, better, stronger and faster. You've got the kind of intangibles we're looking for - the kind we need. I'm not saying that what you did was sustainable, that you could have beaten them over four full quarters. But you don't have to win every battle to win the war. Sometimes you just need to hang on, and that's a victory in and of itself."

"It really wasn't about winning. I just didn't like Paramount thinking he could walk all over us just because most people think he's the second coming."

Mouse laughed at that. "I think I know what you mean."

"Plus, it seems to me that you already have the leadership angle covered. Paramount has that troop of baboons that will follow him over a cliff if he asks them to."

Mouse frowned at that. "Are you saying you're not interested?"

I paused for a moment before responding. "I'm saying that, from my perspective, your problems run a whole lot deeper than lack of leadership."

He looked at me quizzically but didn't say anything, so I went on. "None of you guys seemed to have noticed, but you had a bunch of goons out there ready to pound a group of much-weaker opponents into the sand just because they could. More than that, they enjoyed it! They got a kick out of showing how much muscle they had compared to us."

"I know Paramount went a little far, especially with the Bolt Blast, which he's sorry for-"

"I'm talking about what happened before that. We hadn't finished our game, and he tried to run us off the field. Like he was better than us. Like he was *entitled* to."

Mouse's brow was furrowed deep in thought. This conversation had taken a very serious turn. "Entitlement" was basically a four-letter word when it came to super powers. It's how a lot of supervillains first start out; somewhere along the way they begin thinking that their powers make them better than everyone else. And if you're better than everyone else, then the ordinary rules don't apply to you. And if the rules don't apply, then you're *entitled* to do whatever you want.

After a few seconds of silence, Mouse spoke. "I know it probably looks that way from your point of view, but Paramount probably has more potential than any teen super on the planet. The kids all look up to him, and he's a great leader."

I snorted sarcastically. "They don't look up to him. They're terrified of him. Him and that Gestapo who hang on his every word. Have you noticed that he's built his own little private army to follow him around? He's recruited a gang of thugs, each with the muscle to bench press a city block. There may be potential there, but potential is a pendulum that can swing to either side of the clock – good or bad. I'm on the outside looking in, and even I can see that this will end up very ugly if it's not addressed."

Mouse gave me a hard look. "Who's been training you?"

"Huh?" The question took me by surprise.

"That's a lot of insight for a kid to have. I'm not saying that you're right, but it shows a level of critical thinking that we try to instill in teen supers. But you already have it, which points to training. Long-term, sophisticated, high-level training."

I didn't say anything. Still, he had hit the nail right on the head. It hadn't really come back to bite me in the butt, but I was suddenly nervous that perhaps I'd been trained too well by Gramps and Braintrust.

"Just taking a wild guess," he said when I didn't respond, "I'm assuming you've got a cape in the family - a parent perhaps. Maybe even two."

"Everyone has two parents," I said snarkily, which got a chuckle out of him.

"Look," he added, sobering a little, "I don't think he's the bad seed you take him for, but I'll give some serious thought to your comments about Paramount. But in the meantime, like I said before, not everything is about having super powers. Part of what this little program is set up to do is help us identify some of these other characteristics — things you can't find out from a strength or speed test. "

"Is that how Alpha League found you?" I asked.

Mouse stared at me in silent contemplation for a moment. "People don't know much about me, do they?"

"Not really."

He nodded in understanding. "So what do they say?"

"Not much. You came out of nowhere about two years ago, did something that really impressed the League. So now you're on the team, even though you don't seem to have any powers."

That got another laugh out of him. "Well, between you and me, I really didn't come out of nowhere. See, I went out for the Super Teen Trials three times — and got rejected on all three occasions. My power...well, there's really not a term for what I can do. But suffice it to say that none of the superhero teams at the time saw the value in it because I didn't fit the traditional mold of what they were looking for."

"And now?"

"Now they have a better understanding of what makes a superhero, and they think I have it. And I think you have it."

He stood up. "This year's teen trials are in two weeks. I'll be looking for you there."

He extended his hand and I shook it, implicitly agreeing to attend the trial when a moment before I wouldn't have gone if they begged me. I left the room reflecting on my trial from two years ago, and whether I wanted to risk going through it again.

SENSATION

Chapter 6

The fiasco that turned out to be my tryout for a superhero team had started out innocuously enough. It was two years ago, and I was fourteen at the time - the youngest age at which you could participate in the trials. I had been waiting for this day for years - almost since my powers had first developed and I'd started being trained by my grandfather and Braintrust.

The three of us had jointly agreed that I would attend in a different persona. Even kids who didn't pass the trials often found themselves sparking human interest pieces. In my case, I didn't want anyone poking around in my background for a couple of reasons, first and foremost being that I had wanted to make it on my own, not because of my famous pedigree. If I passed the trials with people knowing who my grandparents were, there would always be the question of whether I'd actually made the cut or if someone had pulled some strings. And if I didn't make it, the embarrassment would just be too great...

In addition, looking into my background would naturally evoke questions about my parents. I wasn't too concerned about my mother; she had jokingly threatened to use any such opportunity to promote her romance novels. However, that would also bring up the subject of my father, and that was a conversation I wasn't ready to have yet.

I chose an appearance loosely based on a high school picture of my grandfather: a tall, gangly but handsome kid, roughly sixteen years old, with a rich chocolate complexion. Moreover, claiming that I was still worried about somebody finding out who I was, I also insisted on completing the persona with a different set of fingerprints and even a different brainwave pattern. (Oddly enough, I didn't even consider being identified by DNA at the time.) BT thought it was idiotic and paranoid to go that far - and he was probably right - but I was persistent. When he finally yielded, BT suggested that instead of dealing with the minutiae of fingerprints, when I shapeshifted I should just do away with prints altogether; my new persona would only leave behind finger*marks*, with no ridge detail.

As to brainwave patterns, the truth of the matter is that I didn't really have any concerns about being identified by such, although it was possible. In all honesty, I had recently developed the ability to control autonomous body functions, like my heart rate, perspiration, etc. BT thought that I could also alter my brainwaves, but my grandfather had forbidden me to experiment in that direction, saying that changing your brainwave pattern could result in a shift in your personality. However, I really wanted to see if I could do it (and what would happen, stupid kid that I was), so I used my desire to remain anonymous during the trials as a pretext for requiring a different brainwave pattern. Although he did so reluctantly, my grandfather eventually gave in.

Following my grandfather's acquiescence, BT explained that - just as I had the ability to speed up and slow down a lot of my bodily functions (like heart rate) - I could also consciously manipulate my cerebral cortex in such a way as to create a different brainwave pattern. In simple terms, brainwaves are electrical impulses in the brain. An individual puts forth different brainwaves based on what he or she is doing: meditating, sleeping, watching an action movie, and so on. Depending on the activity that an individual is engaged in, the pattern of the electrical impulses changes. With BT's help, I was able to conceptualize how everything worked and quickly learned to affect the ebb and flow and even the electrical charge of those impulses, thereby creating a different brainwave pattern for myself. The only problem was that changing my brainwaves was kind of like having a fog in my head. It was as if I was observing myself and everything I did through a haze, though not in a debilitating way. In short, although I didn't realize it initially, this change would cause me to act and react to certain stimuli in a manner that was not typical for me - much as my grandfather had predicted.

Lastly, it had been decided that I would only display one power during the trials. Again, I wanted entry to a team without drawing a lot of scrutiny. Showing up as a jack-of-all-trades super would make me the center of attention. Likewise, displaying any of my more recherché powers would also put me in the spotlight. After a lot of debate, it was settled that I would apply as a flyer. Thus, decked out in my new persona - and a black-and-red costume, complete with cape - I had made my appearance.

The Super Trials have a well-deserved reputation as a complete media circus. Not only are there thousands of hopefuls lined up to register, but there are swarms of reporters and newscasters everywhere. There are actually multiple trials conducted simultaneously across the country, but the one in our town always drew the largest crowds because our city was home base to the Alpha League, who conducted and oversaw the trials for my region.

SENSATION

Technically, the trials consisted of three parts. First, there was registration, which was open to anyone. After registration, all of the candidates would have a chance to demonstrate their powers - one at a time - for the League in private. If they cleared that hurdle, then the real tests would begin. Those who made it through the crucible of the third stage (which usually lasted several days) were typically introduced to the public at a press conference afterwards as new members of the superheroes' Teen Development League. Enrollment at the Academy would follow and eventually - hopefully - a place on a superhero team.

Registration was held outside the League's headquarters, a mid-sized structure in the downtown area that stood as the only building on a large, lush plot of land the size of ten city blocks. There were so many people milling about that I didn't even worry about being seen as I teleported in. Besides, people were showing off their powers left and right: super speed, super strength, telekinesis. It was something that was always great to watch on TV, but seeing it in person - even some of the powers I had myself - was awesome.

Even though they were only in their teens, some of this year's participants were already famous, and the top reporters wasted no time trying to get sound bites from them. There was Dynamo, who had been "outed" earlier in the year when he saved a dozen people from an apartment fire. Vestibule, the striking beauty who already had a career as a teen model was also present and giving an interview to a major network; as the only known teleporter in this year's crop, she was essentially a shoo-in. And then, almost literally standing head and shoulders above everyone else, there was Paramount.

SENSATION

Paramount had displayed super powers almost since the moment he was born. Therefore, not surprisingly, ever since he had reached the age of eligibility, there had been a media frenzy every year as to whether he would "go pro" in terms of entering the Super Trials. But it hadn't happened at age fourteen, or at fifteen. When asked what prompted him to finally toss his hat into the ring, he had given a near-perfect response.

"Just because you have super powers doesn't mean that you're fully qualified to use them," he'd said sheepishly. "To be frank, I had some maturing to do in a lot of ways, and I think the last two years have given me a greater perspective and sense of responsibility - something I didn't really have at age fourteen or even fifteen."

The media ate it up, like hogs devouring slop. Man, I think I even hated him back then - before the disaster my tryout would become.

Despite distractions like Paramount's interview, the registration lines moved along at a nice clip. There were ten lines, and candidates were randomly placed into them. Then you just had to bide your time until you reached the front. The registration tables at the head of each line were manned by former supers and sidekicks.

The guy sitting at the table for my line wasn't anyone that I recognized. He was a short man with a wiry build, wearing glasses and chewing gum. He appeared to be in his fifties, with a receding hairline that was going gray and a thick mustache to match. He had a laptop in front of him that he was typing on intensely as I approached.

"Registration card," he said, holding out his hand. He never took his eyes off the laptop screen.

"Uhhhh…" I stammered. I hadn't even known they'd be giving any out, let alone seen any.

He raised his eyes, deigning to look at me for the first time. "You don't have one?"

"No."

"Not a problem," he said. "We always run out, so half of these yahoos never have one when they get to the front of the line."

He turned back to the screen and began typing again, so he probably didn't notice my relief. (Nor did he seem to notice or care that I was one of the "yahoos" without a registration card.) It would have been a shame if I'd been turned away before I'd even begun because of administrative guidelines.

"Name," he said, impatiently.

I was so lost in my reverie it took me a second to realize that this was the second time he'd actually said it. And I was flummoxed. In all our preparations - coming up with a persona, working on fingerprints, brainwaves, etc. - we had never settled on what name I would use. I stood there in silence for a few seconds, trying to come up with something. Suddenly, a deep baritone sounded behind me.

"He's asking for a name, kid." I didn't have to turn to look; I knew who it was. But I turned anyway, and there he was. Alpha Prime.

It's not every day that you get addressed directly by the world's greatest superhero. He stood a few inches taller than Paramount - more evidence that his son still had a little ways to go before he equaled him. For a big man, he moved rather quietly, the only sound being the slight billow of his cape. Then I remembered that you rarely ever saw him walk; either he zipped around at super speed, flew, or - when not in a rush - he just floated from one spot to another, his superiority and supremacy ever-evident.

"Your name, kid," he repeated, with just a hint of impatience. I felt a sudden fury building, which wasn't typical for me, at the thought of being rushed. I would come to understand later that much of what I said and did over the next few days - particularly at the end - was because I wasn't myself in a certain sense. My altered brainwaves had indeed resulted in some alterations to my personality.

Alpha Prime frowned in concentration. "Do I know you?"

"No," I said with finality. Fist balled in fury, I turned to the guy at the table and - latching on to the moniker I'd just inadvertently been given - angrily stated, "Kid."

"What...?" The guy was clearly taken back by my vehemence.

"Kid," I said again, recognizing my own anger and trying to speak with more civility. "My name is Kid."

The registrar harrumphed and shot me an odd glance before going back to typing. I turned back to the source of my anger, Alpha Prime, but he was gone, floating off through the crowd, shaking hands and wishing everyone good luck.

"Powers?" the registrar said a few seconds later.

"Flight," I replied.

He waited, looking at me expectantly. Finally he asked, "That's it? Flight?"

"Isn't that enough?"

He shrugged. "Suit yourself. Now before I print your name tag, are you sure that this is what you want - 'Kid'?"

"Yeah."

"No 'Kid Flight' or 'Kid Sky' or-"

"Just 'Kid,'" I said. I took the name tag after it was printed and went into the League's headquarters.

****

Inside Alpha League HQ, a large waiting room had been filled with folding chairs for those of us trying out. I took a seat and waited for my name to be called along with thousands of other hopefuls. Basically, when called, we simply had to go into a nearby side room and demonstrate our powers.

I looked at my name tag, which said "Kid-1." I didn't understand the purpose of the numeric designation until later, when a fight broke out between two kids who had both chosen the name "Templar." Apparently, the assistant calling in the next candidate had forgotten to state the number designation, so each Templar thought the other was trying to steal his place in line. Fortunately, the situation was resolved rather quickly, but not before one Templar pulled a glowing sword out of the ether and took a few swings at his adversary who, from what I could see, may not have had any powers at all.

Truth be told, about ninety-five percent of applicants get weeded out at this stage of the trials. Basically, they don't have any powers to speak of, but just want an opportunity to meet a couple of their superhero idols. Another three percent will have negligible powers - abilities that really don't amount to much. (As BT had put it, the ability to float half an inch off the floor and such.) The remaining two percent of participants will constitute the sweet spot among the applicants.

The time passed quickly and quietly for the most part. The one notable event occurred when Paramount came walking through on the way to his test, followed by a gaggle of reporters, all vying to get his attention for a second. As they went past me, one of the reporters on the outskirts of this small mob suddenly stumbled, having snapped a heel on her two-inch stilettos. I reacted quickly, standing up and catching her before she could fall.

"Crap!" she shouted, angrily taking off the shoe and its mate. "As if there wasn't enough going wrong!"

"Sorry," I said. "Next time I'll let you fall."

"What?" She seemed to notice me for the first time. She put a hand up and pulled back her hair. She was in her early twenties, and actually kind of cute. "I'm sorry, not you. Thanks."

"No problem."

"It's just...I really needed a good story here today. This is my last shot." She suddenly looked kind of tearful. "I thought if I could just get a question or two with someone like Paramount, it could get my career back on the right track."

I chuckled. "Unless you've got an audience that numbers in the millions, you can give up on getting anything out of him, or Vestibule, or any of the other household names."

"Great. Just great."

"Hey, if it'll help, you can interview me."

She looked skeptical. "And you are...?"

SENSATION

"Kid," I said. "Just Kid," I added, when she looked like she was expecting more.

"And what makes you so special that we should get you on tape?"

"Because," I said, "in a week, you won't be able to get this interview."

She thought about what that meant. Normally, after the Super Trials, any teens selected were forbidden to give interviews, and media access to them was restricted in the extreme. Interviewing a teen who later made it onto a superhero team was a coup for reporters at these events. Telling her that I wouldn't be available for interviews in the future was dropping a hint that I was someone special.

"Alright," she muttered after deliberating for a few seconds, "but you better be worth it, *kid*." She emphasized the last word, implicating it both as my moniker and as a generic designation. "Sid, let's get set up over here..."

She motioned to someone behind me - a cameraman that I hadn't noticed before. She then had me step over to a nearby wall, which would serve as the background. She ran her fingers through her hair again and then spent a few seconds straightening out her clothes.

Sid held up his hand, palm open. "Ready to go in five, four, three..." He folded his fingers into his fist as he counted down, going silent on the last two digits.

The newswoman gave a beaming smile. "Hi, I'm Sylvia Gossett, reporting to you live from this year's Super Trials. I have with me one of the hopefuls..."

We had about a five-minute interview. As with so many other things that happened then, I don't know what

58

made me go on-camera with her, as I had intended to keep a low profile. (Again, I attribute it to the altered brainwaves.) To this day, however, it remains the only known interview with - and one of only two pieces of film footage containing - the infamous Kid Sensation.

Following the interview, I didn't have to wait long for my name to be called. I was ushered down a short hallway by a pretty redhead who was assisting with registration, and into what was basically a large conference room approximately twenty by thirty feet in size. At one end was an elongated table at which sat three superheroes - two men and one woman: Mouse, Rune, and Esper, each with a laptop in front of them.

Mouse was a fairly new member of the League at that juncture, and as such no one knew much about him - a fact that didn't change much over the next few years.

Rune was an enigma and a true human spectacle. His entire body was covered from head to foot in strange designs: ancient symbols, weird hieroglyphs, obscure characters. He was generally considered to be some type of magician. Because of his appearance, he was one of the less-popular superheroes; speaking bluntly, the runes that covered him gave most people the creeps. Even more disturbing, some of them appeared to be moving.

Esper, the telepath, had a two-fold job here. In addition to observing participants demonstrate their powers, she also took a cursory glance into their brains to make sure that people were who they said they were (i.e., nobody was a supervillain or a mole for one).

"Next contestant," said Rune with a grin, "come on down."

SENSATION

As I approached, I could feel a slight probing into my mind - Esper - and I knew what she'd see. Again, I had been trained by Nightmare, a psychic who - in his prime - had known no equal. As such, I had learned the trick of having a steady stream of male-teenager thoughts running along the surface of my brain: "Cute girl...", "Video games...", "Football..." and the like were on a continuous loop in my head, but outside my mental castle. Satisfied, Esper withdrew from my mind as gently as she had entered, and it's a testament to my grandfather's training that she never knew that I had been aware of her presence.

Mouse looked up from his laptop. "The Kid," he said with a bit of a snort. "It says here you can fly. Let's see it."

I floated up about a foot off the floor, waiting silently as they eyed me.

"Technically, that's not flying," said Rune after an eternity, although it was really about fifteen seconds. "It's floating."

As if to illustrate his point, a pen on the table suddenly floated up into the air. "Or, if you're some kind of fakir, it might even be simple levitation. Flight, on the other hand, implies speed and direction." With that, the pen suddenly began circling around him at a dizzying velocity.

For a second there, I thought he'd said "faker," as if I were a fraud. Even after I realized that he'd said *fakir*, the anger continued building in me. Still airborne, I dashed forward and snatched the circling pen, then flew back to my original position. I held out the pen and then let it drop. I flew to the back of the room and then

60

zoomed back, catching the pen before it touched the floor.

Mouse looked at me stonefaced, while Esper raised an eyebrow in appreciation. Rune clapped his hands and threw his head back in laughter. "I like this kid!" he exclaimed.

I turned and left the room. I didn't really know where I was headed - back to the waiting room, I supposed.

"Hey!" a voice shouted in my direction.

I turned to look and saw the assistant who had shown me into the room. She touched a hand to the side of her head and cocked her head slightly while walking towards me, obviously listening to an earpiece.

"You're in," she said when she got close. "Follow me."

She led me back down the hallway and through another two corridors before stopping at a nondescript door. She took a magnetic key card out of her pocket and slid it through a card reader set in the wall. The door audibly unlocked. I waited, looking at her.

"Go in," she said, raising her hands palm up in exasperated fashion. I opened the door and stepped inside as she walked away, shaking her head and muttering.

I was in another holding area. However, there were decidedly fewer people in here than the previous waiting room. This was the short list, teens with powers or abilities worth looking into a little more. There were chairs arranged in two sections, with an aisle down the middle of them. I took the first seat I came to and sat quietly.

SENSATION

Paramount, of course, was there, the center of attention as usual. I was one of the few who wasn't hanging on his every word. Another was a girl who sat across the aisle from me. She had straight black hair, a smooth complexion, and a simple appearance unadorned by makeup or jewelry. It took me a second, but I quickly recognized her as Electra.

Electra had an unusual backstory. She was allegedly an orphan who the League had found as a baby. Because she exhibited super powers even as an infant, the entire Alpha League had gotten itself appointed as her guardians. She actually lived here at League HQ on one of the residential floors of the building. The only other person who had lived their entire life at League HQ was Paramount, and - like him - she was also expected to be a sure thing as far as being selected by a superhero team.

Over the next thirty minutes a few more people trickled in. Following that, no one came in for the next hour. During all this time, Paramount talked incessantly and inanely about anything that came to mind. Finally though, even he seemed to run out of mindless chatter and sighed grumpily.

"When are we going to get this show on the road?" he asked.

Of course it was a rhetorical question, so we were all shocked when a voice answered.

"Oh, I was just waiting on you to finish. I didn't want to disturb you in the middle of one of your anecdotes."

We all looked to where the voice had come from. In a chair a few rows in front of Electra sat Rune. I didn't recall him being there before, and no one had come into the room. Had he been there the entire time?

SENSATION

Briefly I wondered if he were a teleporter, but quickly decided it didn't matter.

"If you're done, then," he stated, pointedly looking at a now-silent Paramount, "we'll get underway."

Rune stood and cast his gaze about the room.

"You're about to be taken to the next part of the trials. This will be a testing ground where we subject you and your abilities to examination to determine if any of you have the rudimentary requirements to be a superhero."

He closed his eyes, and one of the symbols on his forehead began to glow with a bright, yellow light. Rune began chanting in a language I didn't understand, but with words that intoned power with each syllable. Almost imperceptibly, the room began to vibrate, starting out as a dull hum. Rune's chant continued, but I was surprised to discover that I could now understand the words:

Universe and cosmos, bend to my will;
Make distance between here and there nil;
Time and space rip apart without scar,
May the distant be near, and the near far!

As he spoke, the yellow glow became blinding. The room's trembling grew more violent, and I heard empty chairs vibrating slowly across the floor. I felt an odd sensation, a tugging at my being, as if my body was trying to be two places at once. It wasn't like teleporting; with that, I was simply either here or there, in one place or another. With Rune's spell, and I somehow knew that

63

to be what it was, it was as if I were ubiquitous to a certain extent, and in several places simultaneously.

Then, without preamble, everything came to a halt, and the world normalized again.

"We're here," Rune announced, and then turned and left out the door without further explanation.

Within a few minutes we had all followed him out of the room. Rune had obviously performed some type of trickery, because we certainly weren't at the League's HQ any more.

We were in a gigantic room, with hardwood floors, stone walls, and high arches. Floor-to-ceiling windows gave a panoramic view of a large domed stadium, lush well-manicured lawns, and hundreds of acres of forest. Looking around, I could see that the room was filled with all kinds of games: pool tables, air hockey, table tennis, etc.

Someone tapped me on the shoulder and pointed up. Above the arches was a large sign:

WELCOME TO THE ALL-LEAGUES ACADEMY

Now I knew where we were: the Academy, where heroes-in-waiting got their training - if they were lucky enough to be selected by a superhero team.

"Yes, you are at the Academy," Rune spoke in response to unasked questions. "You will stay here for the next three days while participating in the trials. We have made room for you in the dorms – at opposite ends of the campus, based on gender – and will provide you with a change of clothing for each day's events."

He waved his arm to take in the entire room. "This is the student break room. Whenever you are not being tested, you are free to be in here, or participate in some of the outdoor activities. Tennis, anyone?"

We laughed at this as a glowing blue racket appeared out of nowhere in his hands, and he took a few swings at an imaginary ball.

"Anyway," he continued, as the tennis racket vanished, "you've had a long day, so the rest of the evening is yours. We're fortunate enough to have some student volunteers – who took time out of their own summer break – help us this year."

At this, a number of older teens filed into the room from a nearby hallway.

"These volunteers will show you to your rooms." As he spoke, he began fading, like a ghost winking out of existence. "As I said, you're free to make use of this break room, but I would advise getting a good night's sleep."

And with that, he was gone. I took his advice and, allowing a student volunteer to show me the way, went to my room and went to bed.

****

The trials were basically assessments of our powers. On the first day, they separated us based on our abilities. Out of two hundred of us, there were only seven flyers.

Unless you had another superpower (like super strength), a flyer could usually expect to have a recon role on most super teams. Fly here, scope out this area, report what you see. Your primary role wouldn't be to mix it up with the bad guys (although that happened just as often as not). Thus, the flying trials would be pretty straightforward attempts to gauge qualities such as speed and perception.

The first part of the test involved flying up to a comfortable height (whatever that was for each individual flyer) and then staying there as long as possible. I flew up to what I judged to be about a thousand feet, then stayed there for four hours (or more specifically, until they called me back down). I was proud to see them label my ability to remain aloft as "indefinite."

Next, I had to chase down an aerial drone and manually tag it with a homing beacon. It led me on a merry chase for almost thirty minutes, through wooded areas, around abandoned buildings, and all over the testing grounds. It had been an effort not to display too much speed, but I'd had fun all the same. I had assumed that they were judging my speed, so it was a bit of a shock when, after I was done, the test administrator - a flyer known as Sky High - began asking me odd questions.

"Did you see the bear?" he asked.

"Huh?"

"When you were chasing the drone through the woods, did you see a bear?"

Of course! Being recon, flyers were expected to observe what was going on around them. I went back over the flight in my mind, thinking furiously.

"Yes," I finally answered. "I actually saw two bears - a mother and her cub."

Sky High grunted, apparently surprised, then went on with a barrage of questions that I believe I answered correctly: "Did you see a mailbox...? How many blue cars...? What was the color of...?"

There were other assessments as well, but nothing I found too difficult. In short, over a two-day period, I passed all the tests they put me through. (Or at least I believed I did.)

The third day was just for winding down. The superheroes would discuss and assess the merits of each participant - maybe even meet with a few of them one last time - and let us know at the end of the day if we made the cut. Someone mentioned that there was a paintball range on campus, so a few of us decided to play while we waited.

The Academy's paintball range, although in a well-forested area, was fairly high-tech. Each player could be tagged out by getting hit with a certain number of paintballs. The number of paintballs it took to tag someone out varied based on a computerized assessment of their abilities. For example, the computer would tag me out with seven registered paintball hits. For someone like Paramount, the number was one hundred hits, which was as high as the system would go.

There was a break area set up where teams could rest between rounds. It had lots of refreshments, as well as video screens that carried live broadcasts of teams currently competing. There was lots of good-natured betting on which team would win each faceoff.

There were six of us who decided to play together, three to a team; it was a good match per the computer, which assessed our abilities as being comparable and pegged us all at the same tag-out level. We were in the process of putting on our pads - my team was in blue, the other team was in red - and getting our gear when the prior combatants came into the equipment room. One of the teams included Paramount, who was cheering in obvious victory.

"That was great!" he screamed. "I love it!" I tuned him out as he kept shouting, thinking instead about getting out on the range and discussing strategy with my teammates. We were just getting ready to start our round when the members of the red team approached.

One of them, a telepath called Mindburst, spoke. "We, uh, we, we're going to let those guys take our place this round." He nodded in the direction of Paramount and his team, who stood on the other side of the room, glaring at us.

"Why is that?" I asked.

"Well, they really seem to like it, and we're not really big paintball fans anyway."

This was in direct contradiction to what they had previously said, but it seemed impolitic to mention that at the moment. He and his teammates were clearly nervous and feeling anxious. And that's when I realized the truth: other teens weren't in awe of Paramount. They were afraid of him.

"Suit yourself," I said, shrugging. "But you're missing out on big fun."

With that, I marched out to the paintball range. It didn't occur to me until later that I had never asked my teammates for their opinion on the subject.

The paintball game itself was a serious mismatch. The discrepancy between the tag-out numbers for my team and Paramount's was just too great. There was no way we could win. Nevertheless, we devised the best strategy possible under the circumstances.

The paintball course had several hunting blinds set up in random spots. Each of us would take one, then - using the blind as cover - attempt to shoot the other team whenever they got close. It wouldn't even come close to getting us a victory (we wouldn't be able to shoot them enough times before they got to us), but it was all we had.

I chose an elevated blind, which was basically a little wooden shed sitting on a stand about twelve feet off the ground. A ladder led up to a door cut into the floor of the shed. The door was already open, and when I peeked inside, I saw a family of skunks - a mother and her three young.

I'm no skunk whisperer by any means, and I find it more difficult to interpret the emotions of animals than people. Nevertheless, I could feel the agitation of the mother, whose maternal instincts were kicking into overdrive. I tried to direct feelings of friendship and non-aggression towards her. After a few moments, she seemed to calm a bit - at least enough for me to have a look around.

Inside the blind, rough-hewn, squared-shaped windows had been cut into all four walls. The windows were covered by sheets of plywood hanging down on horizontal hinges. Peeking out, I had clear lines of sight of the other hunting blinds, where my two teammates were hidden.

I telescoped my vision. In short order, things did not go well for either of my teammates. They had each chosen hunting blinds on the ground, and Paramount and his team used the same basic tactic for both of them. They would rush the hunting blind from three sides at once, then fire inside indiscriminately until the person was tagged out.

After my second teammate was tagged out, I started thinking that maybe the hunting blinds weren't such a great idea. One of the baby skunks made a mewling sound, which brought my attention back to them. The skunks were obviously using the place as a den; in fact, the mother may even have given birth here. An idea started taking form in my brain.

Paramount's team was heading my way, having obviously figured out Team Blue's plan to use the hunting blinds. I waited until I was sure they were looking in my direction, then - in a very open and notorious fashion - I lifted the plywood and looked out the window. One of Paramount's teammates saw me and pointed at my hiding place. I quickly lowered the plywood, acting like a kid caught with his hand in the cookie jar.

Turning to the skunks, I spent a few seconds sending a lot of negative emotions towards the mother, who began to make angry noises. Then I slipped out the door in the floor, leaving her riled up.

The foliage around the hunting blind was tall and dense enough that I was sure I couldn't have been seen slipping out. I headed to a nearby bush, away from the direction Paramount's team was coming from, and hid behind it. What occurred next was absolutely classic.

Peeking out from my hiding spot, I saw Paramount and his crew emerge from the trees on the other side of the hunting blind. Paramount held a finger up to his lips, calling for quiet. Then he tapped his thumb to his chest and pointed to the ladder leading up to the shed. His teammates nodded and fanned out as he approached.

I have to admit, for a big guy, Paramount moved with catlike silence and grace. He got to the ladder quickly and slowly climbed up. However, he'd barely had time to stick his head through the door when he suddenly shouted and fell off the ladder. The mother skunk had sprayed him full in the face. The only way it could have been better would have been if his mouth had been open.

Paramount got up screaming and rubbing his face. "A skunk! A skunk!"

His teammates ran to his aid, but began laughing uncontrollably as soon as they understood what had happened. I was in stitches myself, so much so that I didn't even try to run when they closed in on me (my laughter was a dead giveaway) and tagged me out.

Word got out pretty quickly about what had happened. I had completely forgotten that the matches were broadcast back to the break area, so everyone had seen what had happened. (Someone even found the controls and put it on replay.)

I didn't realize it then, but I had done the unforgivable. I hadn't beaten Paramount, which would have been bad enough because the guy really was a sore loser. I had done something far worse: I had embarrassed and humiliated him - made him a laughingstock. And nobody laughs at Paramount. In retrospect, had I known what was to result from that paintball game, I never would have played.

****

That evening, they announced which of us were deemed worthy of entering the Academy. I felt a great sense of relief when my name was called as one of the lucky ones. (Even more, the Alpha League was sponsoring me, so I'd be part of their team of super teens.) Naturally, they called Paramount's name as well. However, he didn't seem to care for the news. He was apparently still fuming about the skunk incident; he gave me the stinkeye (no pun intended) every time he looked my way. And it didn't help that people were still talking about it. (Some kids were even calling him *Polecat*-Mount behind his back.) I slept uneasily that last night.

The next morning is when everything went to hell in a handbasket. Those of us from my region were taken back to the city bright and early (by plane this time, as opposed to Rune's magic), and then brought to a local television station. The plan was to introduce us, one at a time, on a live broadcast as the newest members of the Alpha League Division of the Teen Development League, and as future students at the Academy. Several members of the Alpha League were there to oversee the event: Esper, Buzz (a speedster), Alpha Prime, and Power Piston, an armored hero whose metal suit boasted an impressive array of armaments.

We were all seated on a low stage in a small auditorium, wearing our new Academy uniforms: plain khaki pants/skirts, white zippered shirts, and a cape to top it all off. (We'd been given official Alpha League overnight bags to put our original clothes and personal effects in.) The seats on the stage were just folding chairs arranged in a neat row facing an audience of about three hundred people, mostly reporters and paparazzi. Cameras were placed strategically throughout the place, capturing every angle.

Esper stood at a podium on one side of the stage with Alpha Prime next to her. She called each teen's name, at which point the person would stand up and approach the podium. Esper and Alpha Prime would then pin an emblem - essentially a pledge pin - on the teen's uniform, officially marking them as a teen superhero with Alpha League.

SENSATION

Paramount was seated three chairs away from me. I should have known that something was going to go wrong; menace and malice were emanating off him in powerful waves that were almost palpable. They were emotions I had been feeling from him ever since the paintball game, and they were squarely focused on me. However, I had spent most of the morning trying to ignore him, choosing instead to trade lighthearted jokes with some of the other super teens.

When my name was called, I stood up and walked towards the podium, leaving my overnight bag tucked under my seat. I was a little wary as I went by Paramount, but nothing happened so I felt that he was just stewing. I accepted my pin and was heading back to my seat, waving to the crowd as they applauded. I could still feel acrimony pouring off Paramount like summer heat. Then the emotion changed to something like maniacal glee and satisfaction. That's when Paramount purposely stuck out his foot and tripped me. I was so caught off guard that I actually hit the floor.

I shot an angry look at Paramount as I braced myself and started to rise. He put a hand up to his mouth, as if to hide his snickering. I can't explain what happened next, but fury such as I had never felt - all-encompassing and all-controlling - exploded inside me.

I switched into super speed, moving so fast that later, even on film slowed down as much as possible, my movements were a blur. I grabbed the chair I had been sitting in, and in one smooth motion folded it up, spun around, and hit Paramount with it squarely on the chin in uppercut fashion.

I mentioned before that I don't actually have super strength, but I can mimic it pretty well.

Paramount's head snapped back and he went sailing bodily up into the air. He hit the back wall with an audible smack that shattered plaster, then slid down to the floor.

I stood frozen, still gripping the chair. I seriously doubted that I had hurt him; at only sixteen, Paramount was already practically invulnerable, like his father. The lick I'd just laid on him was probably akin to an adult getting poked in the eye by a baby. It catches you a little off-guard, but it's more irritating than painful, with no lasting effect.

The room suddenly seemed to flash light and dark, like a strobe light on speed. Camera flashbulbs were going off like fireworks during Chinese New Year as photographers in the audience maniacally snapped pictures. And then a freight train hit me.

I was off my feet and on the floor again, this time with the big man himself, Alpha Prime, looming over me. He'd given me a light shoulder bump, relatively speaking, after snatching the chair out of my hands. He stood there, alternating between a somewhat angry look at me and concerned glances at Paramount. In other words, he'd zipped over and put the kibosh on me when it was his jerk of a son, his *bullying* son, his *disgustingly petty* son who had started it all!

I got up breathing heavily and furious, fists balled so tightly it felt as though blood had stopped circulating. Alpha Prime looked at me without concern over his welfare.

"You don't want to fight me, son," he said. "It'll be over like that." He snapped his fingers in my direction.

"Oh, I know," I hissed, totally incensed. "Like that." I snapped my fingers – and Alpha Prime disappeared.

SENSATION

I had teleported him; I knew that much. But I hadn't intended to, hadn't even known I was about to do it. I didn't even know where I'd sent him. Unfortunately, I didn't have time to dwell on it, because in the next few seconds I had the fight of my life on my hands and for the first time I was truly able to put to use the years of training I had been given.

Everyone had frozen when Alpha Prime disappeared, and there were shocked gasps from both the audience and the stage. Buzz was the first to recover. He had actually been at the back of the auditorium, near the exit doors. He came zooming down the aisle at full speed. You didn't need to be psychic to realize that he was in attack mode.

I reached out and mentally grabbed his ankle, telekinetically tripping him much as Paramount had physically done to me. Suddenly he was a flailing mass of arms and legs tumbling end-over-end at Mach speed. He slammed into the lower portion of the stage with bone-jarring force.

I felt a smug satisfaction at having stopped him, but the feeling was short-lived as someone applied a crow-bar to my brain. *Esper.* Recognizing them now as a feint, she'd scattered the cursory thoughts I generally keep on the surface of my mind and forced her way into my mental castle, ready to wreak havoc.

Straining with the effort of mentally fighting, I turned towards her. Her brow was furrowed and her eyes glowed as she focused on trying to mentally incapacitate me. Suddenly she drew in a sharp breath. The glow left her eyes and her face went slack. Then her body went stiff as a board and she fell over backwards, as if participating in some sort of trust exercise - only no one was there to catch her. She hit the floor like a plank of wood.

I smiled inwardly. Esper had fallen into the mental equivalent of a trapdoor in my mind. *My brain, my rules.* However, she was a powerful psychic. My trick would only work once, and it wouldn't work for long.

The sound of hydraulics and the whirr of machinery in motion brought me back to myself. Power Piston had stood up and was pointing some kind of weapon at me. I moved at super speed as he fired.

A small ball came out of the weapon's nozzle. It looked crumpled and oddly shaped, but slowly expanded into a semicircle of mesh. I recognized it as Power Piston's taser net. It would wrap around a target and then emit a charge to shock it into submission.

Still in hyper-speed mode, I stepped aside as the net came towards me. As it went past in what appeared to be slow motion from my point of view, I reached out and grabbed the ends of it with both hands. Pivoting, I then spun around and flung the net back at its point of origin. It wrapped around Power Piston, then dispersed its electrical charge. I could hear the person in the suit of armor scream, and then the armor appeared to shut down, its circuits apparently overloaded.

I looked around. All the League members present were down. (Correction: I saw Buzz's gloved hand come up over the edge of the stage, meaning he'd be up in a minute.) Paramount was getting to his feet again, and the other teens on stage were trying to figure out whether to fight or not. Not that it mattered; I was ready to put them all down for the count. It hadn't even been a minute since Paramount had tripped me, and I wasn't even out of breath.

SENSATION

That's when I realized things had gone horribly wrong. Was I really ready to go toe-to-toe with these kids who I was just joking with an hour ago? We had somehow veered down the wrong path if that were indeed the case.

Just like that, my anger began dissipating. I needed to get out of there. My overnight bag was still on the floor where I'd left it. I teleported it into my hand, slung the strap over my shoulder, and took a step towards one of the stage walls, preparing to phase through, when a stick of mental dynamite went off in my head. Esper again, I realized. The force she'd applied before was a love tap compared to what she was doing now.

Caught unprepared, I staggered to the side under the pressure of Esper's attack. I put out a hand to steady myself, presumably against a wall but instead came up against something else, firm but yielding. I looked and saw that it was actually a person who I had come up against - Electra. Then I saw where my hand had landed on the front of her uniform. *Not good, dude...*

Electra drew in a deep, shuddering breath. Then she screamed. Not the movie scream of a woman in danger, or the scream of someone facing complete frustration, or even the scream of a person in unimaginable pain. It was a scream of a teenage girl (and belted out as only a teenage girl can) of complete and utter angst and despair, a scream that voiced every emotion in the spectrum, stating I-hate-you-how-could-you-why-me-I-hate-life-I'm-so-embarrased-let-me-just-die-you're-awful-I'll-kill-you...

As Electra let out her long, undulating, bloodcurdling shriek, the air became ionized. I felt the hair on my head and arms begin to stand up. Little bolts of lightning crackled through the air around her, and several of the overhead lights blew out in showers of hot, glowing sparks. People in the audience began screaming and running. I felt Esper shift her concern from my mind over to Electra, trying to calm her. It didn't seem to be working.

I phased, becoming insubstantial as Electra pointed in my direction. An arc of electricity shot out from her fingertips, passed through me and struck... Paramount. Apparently he had launched himself at me while I'd been distracted, only to get shocked for his trouble. He screamed in anguish as the electricity shot through him and knocked him back against the wall, much to my amusement.

I teleported behind Electra. I kicked her legs out from under her, and her bottom hit the floor with a thud. Grabbing her by her cape, I dragged her to a nearby wall. I made the wall insubstantial, pulled her cape through it, then solidified it again. Then I teleported to the other end of the stage.

Everyone - Esper, Buzz, the other teens - was rushing towards Electra, who was struggling to get to her feet but couldn't; she had no leverage due to the height at which her cape was stuck in the wall. Again, I felt anger welling up in me. I was the one who had been attacked - by almost everyone - and nobody seemed concerned for my welfare. I put my fingers to my lips and gave a shrill, heads-up whistle. Everyone turned to look in my direction. I flipped them the bird, then phased through the wall.

I came out on the street outside the studio. People were still fleeing the building, so concerned for their own welfare that no one had noticed me yet. That wouldn't last long, though, since I was still in the Academy uniform. I changed my appearance to that of a young punk rocker with spiked hair. I reached up to unzip the Academy shirt, and as I did so my hand touched the pledge pin. In fury, I yanked it out and flung it to the ground. Then I stomped on it.

There was a small crackle of electricity beneath my foot. I reached down and picked up the crushed pin, then telescoped my vision to take a closer look at it. I saw a small spark in the mangled remains, but also loads of circuitry and wiring. The spark died, and a tiny wisp of smoke rose up. More out of curiosity than anything else, I shoved the pin into my pants pocket, then quickly removed the Academy shirt and cape, flinging them into a nearby garbage bin.

There was a hot dog vendor on the corner, and I had used up copious amounts of energy in my fight. Pulling out the little cash I'd brought to the Super Trials from the overnight bag, I approached and ordered three chili dogs, wolfing them down in record time. Then I ordered three more. I was eating the last of them when someone shouted something and everyone started to look up. I followed suit, and saw a streak of black and gold zooming towards the studio. Alpha Prime. As he approached, a noise like a thunderclap rang out through the atmosphere, the telltale sound of a sonic boom as he dropped down to subsonic speed. He had clearly been moving at a record pace in order to get back here. It wasn't until later that I found out - courtesy of various news reports - where I had teleported him:

Bobby Trione's treehouse.

SENSATION

Chapter 7

My on-camera fight with the Alpha League became one of the most-watched pieces of film of all time. As the only person to have an interview with me, Sylvia Gossett was propelled to overnight stardom and became host of her own nationally syndicated show. Braintrust examined the League pin I had received and eventually determined that it read and tracked biometric data, among other things, about the wearer. In short, from the second I put it on, it had gathered and relayed information about every power that I used.

As for me, some people said that I was a criminal who viciously attacked the League on national TV. However, the general consensus among the public was that Paramount had started the fight by tripping me. One headline read, "Kid Puts Up Sensational Fight Against Alpha League!" Although I hadn't made a public appearance as Kid since then, the media (and the general public thereafter) had taken to referring to me as -

"Kid Sensation," said a sudden voice out of nowhere.

I looked up and saw a girl, Electra, approaching me. Lost in thought about my prior tryout, I hadn't even noticed that I had wandered back to the Academy's student break room.

"What...?" I stammered, still in shock at the name she'd addressed me by.

"Kid Sensation," she repeated, stopping right in front of me. "You should remember that name."

I'm sure I must have looked bewildered.

"Paramount has had it in for Kid Sensation ever since their run-in," she went on. "Of course, he takes everything as an insult, so that's a pretty long list, and your little stunt on the football field may have put you on it."

"So now I've got to worry about Para-Jerk coming after me?" I wondered out loud. "That guy really is a loose cannon."

"He's got some issues," she agreed. "But you've got to understand: he's the son of the world's greatest superhero. He's under constant scrutiny all the time, as well as pressure to live up to his father's name."

"So I should feel sorry for him because he has a bunch of A-Level super powers and he's expected to use them for good?"

"No, but I just want you to try to understand him a little."

"You sure seem to be defensive of him. Much more than I'd be of my friends." I left the rest unsaid.

She laughed. "Are you trying to ask me if he's my boyfriend?"

"Is he?"

More laughter. "No way. We grew up together. He's like my brother."

Somehow, that gave me an odd sense of relief — and satisfaction. The conversation then changed to more mundane matters and chitchat: the superheroes we admired most, what our home lives were like, our friends, etc. She seemed fascinated by everything I had to say, and we actually spent the rest of the day in each other's company. Unfortunately, the rest of the day turned out not to be very long; thanks to Paramount's outburst on the football field, the day's events got shut down early and we were on our way back by four o'clock.

SENSATION

We sat next to each other on the return trip, still talking. In the back of my brain, however, I was trying to find an excuse to see her again. She nixed the idea of going to the Natural History Museum the next day (she'd already seen the current exhibits), and also shot down my suggestion of going to the zoo (she didn't like the idea of animals in cages). At that point, I was ready to take the hint when she suddenly caught me off guard.

"Are you doing anything later tonight?" she asked.

Too surprised to say anything, I just shook my head no.

"Well, a couple of us are going to see the new *Starcrosser* movie. Do you want to come?"

"Sure!" I practically shouted, completely overeager and with what was surely a stupid grin on my face.

"Great!" She blurted out an address that I automatically memorized and repeated back to her. "You can pick me up at seven."

I stared off into space, momentarily struck dumb by what she had said.

Pick her up at seven?

Pick her up?

As in *drive*?

SENSATION

Chapter 8

My grandfather was laughing so hard that tears were rolling down his cheeks.

"It's not funny!" I screamed, although in truth it was somewhat comical.

I had a hot date with a pretty girl in just a few hours, and I was going to ruin it before it even got started. Despite all my powers, all my abilities, all the things I could do, I had failed to complete a pivotal rite of passage for teens. I had never learned to drive.

Speaking frankly, it was a skill I had never needed before. If I needed to be somewhere, I could either teleport or run there. A car, for me, was a slow method of transport. Now my arrogance was coming back to haunt me.

"I'm sorry," my grandfather said between chuckles, "but I just can't teach you how to drive in" - he glanced at his watch - "two hours."

At that point, I left my grandfather's apartment in disgust and turned to Braintrust, calling him in desperation. Unfortunately, he was of the same opinion as my grandfather: there just wasn't enough time to teach me.

"However, I do have some good news," BT added. "I was able to get some information on your stalker."

For a moment I was confused about what he meant, and then it dawned on me. "Oh, Pinchface."

"Yes. His name is actually Reilly Kubosh. He's a finder."

"What does that mean?"

"He finds things - people for the most part. Tracks them down."

"How?"

"No one knows. My understanding is that he has some sort of power that helps him. Maybe it's smell, maybe he's psychic...who knows?"

"How'd he get on to me?"

"It's hard to say, but from what I've been able to learn, he needs a starting point. He needs to know either where his target's been or where he's going to be. But after he crosses the target's path, he's locked onto them and can't be shaken off."

"Is he dangerous?"

"Not from what I've learned. Maybe he just wants the reward."

"In that case, why wait until now to go for it? That reward's been out there for a while."

"Again, maybe he didn't have a starting point before."

"So the question is, who gave it to him?"

I got off the phone with Braintrust and pondered the mystery of Reilly Kubosh. After a few minutes, I gave up on it and went back to what was really important: my date. I returned to begging my grandfather to teach me to drive.

"You have to," I pleaded. "I don't have any other options."

"There are always options, Jim," was his reply. "Let's just see what we've got here."

As usual, Gramps was right. After discussing the matter, it seemed that I actually had three options: (1) have my mother or grandfather chauffeur us around all evening; (2) allow Gramps to enter my brain and "take control" during the times when I was behind the wheel such that he would actually be driving; or (3) take a cab. The first option was completely unacceptable. The second was almost as bad; the thought of Gramps running around in my brain during my date gave me the heebie-jeebies. That left the third; not ideal, but any port in a storm.

****

Before I left, my mother insisted on seeing me. It was my first real date, I suppose, and - despite constantly encouraging normal behavior on my part - she seemed a little nervous, as if maybe she didn't want me to go.

"Just watch yourself," she said. "Be careful."

"Be careful of what?" I asked. "I'm just going on a date, not trying to catch a supervillain."

"Some girls can trap you a lot easier than a supervillain. Not all of them can be trusted. And even smart guys have a tendency to be stupid around certain girls - especially if they're pretty."

I gave her a hug and left, not fully understanding everything that she'd said.

****

Electra didn't seem to mind a cab at all. I simply told her that my car was in the shop and she accepted my explanation without question. She looked great, choosing to wear form-fitting black jeans and a light blue blouse. Although she had mostly foregone makeup again, she did have on a luscious shade of red lipstick. On my part, I chose to wear jeans and a golf shirt.

SENSATION

The house where I picked her up wasn't where she lived, of course. However, she didn't like the idea of being picked up for a date at League HQ (and I didn't blame her), so she used a friend's address.

We met her other friends at the movie theater. There were two other couples (to the extent Electra and I could be considered a "couple"), all of whom I recognized as teen supers. A big guy named Herc who was a super-strong brawler but not the sharpest knife in the drawer intellectually. His date was a brown-skinned beauty named Aqua who had some sort of water power. The other couple consisted of a fellow named Nemesis who could turn other supers' powers against them and a waifishly thin girl called Rapunzel, who could use her ankle-length hair like additional limbs.

The movie was okay, but nothing to really write home about. The storyline involved an intergalactic hero's efforts to stop a plot that could destroy the universe. It seemed to contain the requisite number of explosions, fistfights, and other eye candy, so I'm sure it met with general expectations.

Truth be told, however, the movie had less than my full attention. I spent a good portion of the time trying to act in a manner that was completely natural but which would, at the same time, let me either hold Electra's hand or put my arm around her. She was apparently a seasoned expert at avoiding both. If I tried to take her hand, it would be at that juncture that she reached into the bucket of popcorn that I'd bought. If I tried to put my arm around her shoulders, she'd choose that moment to turn around and say something to Aqua and Herc, who were seated behind us (and seeming to have a good laugh at my expense).

SENSATION

After the movie, we went to a nearby diner for something to eat. The waitress was kind enough to seat us at a big circular table that could easily accommodate large parties.

After taking our seats, the conversation turned surprisingly in my direction.

"So," said Aqua, "tell us a little about yourself, Jim."

"Not much to tell," I said noncommittally. "I'm sixteen, I'm in high school, I like sports, yada, yada, yada."

Everyone snickered a little at that, but Aqua was undeterred.

"There's got to be more to you than that," she said. "It's not everybody who gets the best of Paramount."

Nemesis leaned forward conspiratorially. "That was you? No way! I wish I'd been there to see it!"

I was a little surprised. "You've heard about it?"

"It's all kids have been talking about today," Rapunzel piped in. "Especially the girls."

"Girls?" I said, shocked.

"Oh yeah," Aqua noted. "In fact, a couple of them were a little peeved when Electra staked her claim on you for the rest of the afternoon."

I looked at Electra, whose face was impassive. All of this was news to me.

"So, since you're off the market," Aqua continued, "I suppose the next question is: are there any more like you at home?"

"Hey!" Herc interjected jealously, smacking his palm on the table hard enough to rattle dishes, silverware and everything else. I didn't even realize he was smart enough to be following the conversation. As I said, he wasn't the sharpest knife in the drawer, but he obviously wasn't the butter knife either.

"No, baby. It's not like that." Aqua rubbed Herc's muscular forearm soothingly. "I have an identical twin sister," she said in explanation.

"Really?" Electra finally joined the conversation. "In the two years I've known you I've never heard you mention her."

"Well, we don't really speak," Aqua said, eyes cast down. Then she burst into a small fit of laughter that took us all by surprise. "Sorry," she said, looking around the table. "Private joke."

****

Dinner was an interesting affair, with several people around the table demonstrating their powers. Rapunzel, whose hair was actually stronger than steel, used her locks to juggle a few utensils; she also bent a knife in two, then straightened it back out. Aqua, a practical joker, had a habit of making the water in each of our glasses disappear via evaporation just when someone was preparing to drink it.

After we finished eating, Nemesis offered to pick up the tab. (He apparently came from a wealthy family, and didn't mind splurging on his friends.) While he settled the bill, I spoke with the hostess about calling a cab. After being assured that a taxi passed by the diner every few minutes, we all went outside. We were in the midst of saying our goodbyes - girls kissing each other on the cheek, guys shaking hands - when Electra suddenly became bright-eyed.

"I've got an idea," she said. "Why don't we go back to the League Headquarters and show Jim around? Give him the ten-cent tour?"

"No," Aqua began, making me feel she was about to decline. "I think we're going to—"

An odd look passed between her and Electra.

"Actually, that sounds like a great idea," Aqua declared, completely reversing course. "You guys can ride with us in Herc's car."

The significance of what had just happened wasn't lost on me. I took it to mean that Electra didn't want to end the night alone with me, another indication that this date had not gone well in her mind. I suddenly wanted to be somewhere else. Anywhere else.

"That sounds nice," I began, "but it's getting late and I know you all probably want to get home. I can get the tour some other time." I glanced at my watch in a blatantly obvious manner. "Plus, I just remembered there was something I was supposed to do, so I might even have to put Electra in a cab by herself."

I looked at Electra with pleading in my eyes, hoping that she understood and would take the out I was offering.

Please, don't embarrass me. I get the message; I won't bother you again. You won't have to spend a nanosecond more than necessary in my presence. Just let me leave here with some dignity.

Electra's mouth opened as if she were going to say something. I felt sure she was going to retract her suggestion of a tour, but Aqua didn't give her a chance.

"Whatever you've got going on, it can wait," Aqua said, hooking her arm into mine and pulling me along. "Plus," she whispered so only I could hear, "it can't be more important than spending time with a pretty girl." Then she winked at me and giggled.

****

Conversation on the drive back to League HQ was dominated by Aqua, who had a totally vivacious personality. Herc drove a large SUV, which befitted someone of his size. Nemesis and Rapunzel followed closely behind us in his car, an expensive import that Nemesis had received as a present on his last birthday.

Getting into the headquarters was a bit of a trial and required going through a series of rigorous checkpoints. As teen members of the Alpha League, everyone in the two cars (except me) had parking privileges. The building boasted an underground parking garage, for which the only means of ingress and egress was a huge armored door that opened by sliding on horizontal tracks. The door opened automatically as we approached and both vehicles entered. Glancing backwards, I saw the door close surprisingly fast behind Nemesis' car.

Fifty yards or so ahead was another armored door; it suddenly occurred to me that between the door in front of us and the one behind, we were trapped in a small, enclosed space. I mentioned as much to Electra.

"Security," she replied. "We take it very seriously around here, and the garage is probably one of the weak points so the League has taken precautions." She pointed ahead of us, where a keypad and screen sat on the wall next to the door. As we got closer, turret guns in the upper corners of the room swiveled, barrels tracking our car. I also noticed cameras placed strategically around the room.

About ten feet from the door, Herc came to a stop.

"I'll take care of it," Aqua said, jumping out of the vehicle. She ran up to the keypad and punched in some digits I couldn't see.

"She has to enter a code for us to get in," Electra explained.

"And a print scan," she said when Aqua placed her palm on the screen.

"And a password," she noted as Aqua muttered something I couldn't hear.

"And a retinal image," Electra said with finality, watching Aqua lean towards the screen while a jittery light shined in her eyes.

Aqua ran back and got into the car as the second armored door slid seamlessly open.

****

After parking, we had to pass through three more security checkpoints before we actually made it into the main building. Following that, the rest of our party began showing me around.

The League Headquarters was a mid-rise of about twenty-five stories. The top five floors were designated as living quarters for the team (including teen members), but those were generally off-limits to visitors. Likewise, most of the other floors were considered "League Eyes Only." In short, the tour that Electra promised me was primarily confined to the team's museum, which occupied a good portion of the ground floor.

SENSATION

The museum essentially consisted of a long corridor known as the Hall of Heroes, with statues of all the former and current League members. There were rooms located on both sides of this hallway, each with its own particular theme. For instance, there was a room known as Highlight Hill, with photos and artists' renditions of the League's most famous battles. There was also a memorial room, for those heroes who had fallen in combat.

Electra and the others were good tour guides, but frankly speaking, there was nothing special about what they were showing me. It wasn't anything more than the regular tour that just about everybody in the city had gone on at some time or another - including me, on numerous occasions. The only thing that got my blood pumping were the statues of my grandparents, Nightmare and Indigo, which stood facing across from each other in the Hall. Aside from that, I didn't really see what the big deal was - especially since I didn't want to be here in the first place. (On a side note, although my father was here as well, on this occasion I chose to deliberately ignore any semblance of him in the museum, much as he had ignored me all my life.)

"This has been great," I finally said, trying to sound more interested than I felt, "but I should probably get going."

"Okay, but there's something else I want to show you," Electra said, tilting her head for me to follow her. "Something special."

She led us out of the museum and through the main lobby to another door near the back of the room. A sign next to the door read "League Members Only." Electra punched in a code on a keypad next to the door. She didn't seem to care whether I saw the code or not. A red light flashed on the pad, accompanied by an irritating buzz.

"Uggh," Electra groaned, frustrated. "They changed the code again. Anybody remember what the new code is?"

I turned to look at the rest of our ensemble, all of whom shook their heads.

"Great," Electra muttered, "that's just great."

I was suddenly curious. I turned to Aqua, who was behind me. "They change the codes a lot around here?"

Aqua nodded, saying, "Every week on interior locks; every two weeks on exterior ones, like the garage."

"So what now?" I asked. "Are we done?"

"Not exactly," Aqua said with laughter in her voice. "Why don't you turn around and watch your girl do her thing."

If the "my girl" comment affected Electra in any way, she didn't show it. In fact, I'm not even sure she heard it. She was holding her hand out towards the door and frowning in deep concentration. I began to feel an ionized charge slowly building in the air. I involuntarily took a step back, having previously been an eyewitness to the type of power Electra had.

There was a slight crackle of electricity and then I saw little shoots of lightning zipping across the surface of the door. Abruptly, there was the sound of tumblers moving and the audible click of a lock changing position. Then the door opened.

"Voila," said Electra, turning to us with a flourish.

We hustled inside quickly and found ourselves in a stairwell leading down. As we descended, I asked Electra what she had done to the door.

She paused in thought for a second as we walked. "How much do you know about electronics and magnetism?" she asked.

"Not much," I answered truthfully.

"Well, let's just say it was a magnetic lock but I was able to electronically bypass the code requirement."

At the bottom of the stairwell we came to another locked door, which Electra opened in the same manner as the first. She and the others then led me down a complicated series of hallways - practically a maze - before stopping at a set of elevator doors. Electra used her powers again to get the doors to open.

As we stepped inside, I noticed that there were no buttons to push; apparently there was only one place you could go in this elevator. The doors closed and the elevator started descending. No one said anything, but I saw nervous glances between the others. When I opened myself empathically, I felt nervousness and anxiety from several of them - as well as something like determination from Electra.

Rapunzel finally spoke. "Electra, do you really think we should—"

"It's fine," Electra snapped, cutting her off. "It's not a problem."

I wondered what was going on but kept my mouth shut. I wasn't clear on what was happening, but I was suddenly interested.

We rode the rest of the way down - about another ten seconds - in silence. The elevator's momentum slowed and, after coming to a complete stop, the doors opened with a slight hiss.

As we stepped out of the elevator, I noticed that we were in some kind of lobby, about fifteen by twenty feet in area. Long hallways stretched off to both the left and the right, as well as directly ahead of us. All around us I could hear mechanized drones and hums, the sounds of large machinery in operation.

Electra led the way down the hallway to the right. "Come on."

We all followed - the others sheepishly. They obviously knew more about what was going on than I did. About midway down the hall, Electra stopped and opened a doorway to her left.

The room we went into was large and spacious. Along one side was a huge expanse of what was obviously extremely sophisticated - and expensive - computer equipment. There weren't a lot of flashing lights and dials, but there were quite a few screens and monitors. Along the other wall were what appeared to be a number of huge open stalls. The walls for each went from floor to ceiling. Looking into the nearest one, I could see a cot against one wall, a sink and a chair. From this angle, they all looked like jail cells (albeit cells with an open front instead of bars). Then it hit me.

These were cells! *Nullifier* cells! I was about to make a comment to that effect when someone else suddenly spoke.

"What are you kids doing here?" It was Mouse, quietly looking at one of the computer screens and taking notes. He was wearing black trousers and a black t-shirt. I wondered how I hadn't noticed him before.

SENSATION

"You know you aren't supposed to be here," he continued without looking up.

It was Electra who responded. "We just wanted to show Jim the nullifier cells."

"Oh, hey," Mouse said, looking up and seeming to notice me for the first time before becoming engrossed in his work again. "Electra, I'm sorry; you'll have to impress your date later. We're in the middle of an operation."

"Please, Mouse," Electra pleaded. "We'll just take a quick look at one of the cells and leave."

"Fine." Mouse waved his hand in irritation. "Just make it quick."

We all hustled over to the nearest cell. Most people never get to see a nullifier, so it occurred to me that I needed to look somewhat awestruck. Silently, I was counting my blessings that Mouse had spoken up earlier and kept me from blurting out that I knew what it was.

There was a small panel, almost like a podium, at the front of each cell. Electra pressed a number of buttons on the panel for the cell where we had congregated, and a soft hum filled the air. I felt a pressure building at the front of the cell - almost imperceptibly at first, then slowly growing. Looking intently, I saw a concave shape, ghostly white in color but still transparent, slowly take form at the cell entrance. I didn't fully realize what it was until Electra stepped over and leaned against it.

"A force field!" I said, almost crying out.

"Pretty cool, huh?" Electra asked. "Come touch it."

I walked over next to Electra and gently reached my hand out until I felt something. The force field was somewhat yielding, allowing me to exert a little bit of pressure on it. Then it pushed back, shoving my hand away like a spring under pressure.

I'd been around force fields in the past (often in BT's lab), but I'd never actually *seen* one before, because force fields were typically invisible.

"Where does the color come from?" I asked.

"It's artificial," she replied. "If you work around force fields long enough, you'll eventually run into them. From what I understand, it's like being hit with a punch that you never see coming. It's worse than an ordinary punch, because it's completely unexpected and you don't have time to brace yourself. Making it visible prevents those kinds of mishaps."

I nodded in understanding, and Electra laughed a little. Turning to her friends, she said, "Okay, Aqua, turn it off."

She must have still been leaning on it somewhat, because when the force field went off Electra stumbled a little into the cell. I instinctively reached forward and caught her, as she reflexively extended her hand and grabbed at my arm. She got her balance back after a second, but - much to my surprise - didn't move away.

"Aren't you a gentleman," she said, with her hand still on my arm. She looked into my eyes, and in a moment I was completely lost as she tilted her head up and leaned towards me. I closed my eyes and inclined my head. I heard a sudden gasp from either Rapunzel or Aqua, but I didn't care. I just wanted to kiss the girl in front of me.

And just when I thought our lips were about to touch, someone hit me in the chest with a sledgehammer.

Chapter 9

I was momentarily dazed and struggled to get back to my feet. I was also having a hard time catching my breath, having had the wind knocked completely out of me. I glanced around and saw that I was at the back of the nullifier cell. I rubbed my chest where I'd been hit and felt something warm. Looking down, I noticed a scorch mark on the front of my shirt; it was still smoking. It was then that I realized what had happened.

Electra had blasted me. Judging from where I picked myself up off the floor, her power had blown me all the way to the back of the cell. When I had leaned in thinking of an electri*fying* kiss, she'd been thinking about electro*cuting* me. Apparently, my mother was right. Guys *are* stupid, and some girls *can't* be trusted. It was so comical I almost laughed. So much for this date.

I tried to teleport. Nothing happened. That's when the full import of everything hit me. Not only was I in the nullifier cell, it was on and in full effect! At the front of the cell, I saw that the force field was in operation, too. Through it, I could see Electra apparently arguing vigorously with Mouse and the other four teens. Their voices were loud, but I couldn't make out the words so I walked to the front of the cell until I could understand what was being said.

"...this while we're in the middle of an op to get Kid Sensation!" Mouse was saying.

"You don't need an op to find Kid Sensation!" Electra retorted, before gesturing wildly in my direction. "He *is* Kid Sensation!"

"And just how do you know that?" Aqua asked.

"His bioelectric field!"

98

SENSATION

"What?" Nemesis responded, confused. At this point, I was interested myself, so I moved even closer.

"His body's bioelectric field," Electra slowly repeated. "Everybody has one."

"So what?" Aqua asked.

"She can sense them," Mouse responded, before Electra could speak. "Bioelectric fields. It's part of her power."

He turned and looked at me before continuing. "With her, a bioelectric field is as good as a picture or a fingerprint. She can identify somebody with it the way you and I can pick people out of a lineup."

I couldn't help but laugh this time. All that crazy stuff that I'd gone through to maintain my anonymity: shapeshifting, removing fingerprints, altering brainwaves...and then someone just identifies me by my bioelectric field.

"What's so funny?" Herc queried, but I ignored him and kept right on laughing. Mouse turned his attention back to Electra, ignoring me for the moment.

"You say that he's Kid Sensation," he began. "Assuming he is, when did you figure that out?"

"Today, at the football game," she replied. "I knew as soon as I got close enough to him to feel his field."

"Well, why didn't you tell anybody, instead of going through all this?" He made an expansive gesture that took in me, the cell, and more. I sobered up at this, my laughter dying away; here was an explanation I wanted to hear.

"Because he reads minds!" she exploded. "I've been trying to keep my thoughts penned up all day, the way Esper taught me, in case he was listening in, and covering up what I was really thinking with stupid things like how I hoped it would be a good movie, and how cute he is, and how I want butter with my popcorn, and-"

"Wait a minute," I interjected. They all turned to look at me, as it was the first time I'd spoken since I got locked in the cell. "You think I'm cute?"

Electra grunted in irritation, then turned back to Mouse without giving me the courtesy of an answer.

"Bottom line: I tried not to think about it because he might be listening in. I tried not to get too close because Esper says contact or even close proximity increases the possibility of a telepath being able to read you. Plus he can teleport and phase through walls. Basically, I didn't tell anybody because I never knew when he might be eavesdropping. So I came up with this plan."

Mouse rubbed his chin, nodding and staring blankly into the air - apparently in deep thought. He seemed to buy her explanation, because he now turned his attention to me.

"Well," he said. "There's a lot of logic to what she's said. Moreover, there's the fact that since you've been in that cell, your face has changed."

Oh jeez! My hand went to my face instinctively. I'd completely forgotten that I had made some alterations.

"It hasn't changed a lot," Mouse continued, "but certainly enough to be noticeable."

I was in shock. This night had quickly devolved into something unrecognizably horrible. And earlier I couldn't imagine how this date could have gotten any worse. I almost started laughing again at the irony of the situation.

SENSATION

"Listen," Mouse said, "I'm not asking whether or not you're Kid Sensation. We're actually in the middle of an op right now to locate him - an op that's based on excellent information - so I don't know how much of anything I just heard is true. I just want to talk to you about this situation."

He looked at me as if he expected a response. When I didn't give him one, he went on. "With that understanding, if I turn off the nullifier, do I have your word that you'll give me a minute of your time to discuss this?"

I pretended to think about it, but it's not like I had a lot of choice. I wasn't going anywhere as long as I was in this cell and the nullifier was on. Plus, I was curious about this op they were running. After a few moments, I nodded my head in assent.

Mouse reached over and turned off the force field and the nullifier. Just as a test, I teleported out of the cell and right next to him. It probably removed any doubt as to who I was, but I was no longer planning on just walking out of this place anyway.

If having me pop into existence right next to him was startling in any way, Mouse did an excellent job of not showing it.

"Clock's ticking." I tapped my watch.

Mouse wasted no time. "Look, what happened following the trials two years ago wasn't your fault—"

My laughter, harsh and resolute, cut him off. "You think I blame myself for what happened? You think I've been moping around with guilt like I did something wrong? It was the League's pet monster Paramount who started it."

101

SENSATION

"We know that," he admitted, not trying to argue, "just like we know that the team members who were there probably didn't respond as they should have. But they thought they were in the presence of a threat. After all, the first thing most of them saw was you walloping Paramount. Then you did who-knew-what to Alpha Prime."

As always, just thinking about what had happened made me angry. In my head, I had longed for the day that I could call the League on the carpet for what had happened, but right now I was struggling just to control my temper. I glanced at Electra and her friends, but nobody said anything. A couple of them even looked away.

When it became clear that I wasn't going to respond, Mouse went on. "The bottom line is that nothing that happened should be construed as something that would have kept you from being one of us. And frankly speaking, we could use you right now. There are some things going on–"

Mouse stopped abruptly as the air in the room suddenly shimmered, and a hologram of Esper appeared.

"Mouse, this is Esper. We're at the target location."

"It's okay," Mouse responded. "I've got new information on the target. We can call off the op."

"I don't think we can do that. We've got a situation here. You need to see this."

"Okay, expand the hologram to panoramic view."

I watched for a few seconds as the scene began to expand. Then I reached out and tapped Mouse on the shoulder.

"Minute's up," I said.

SENSATION

"No, wait—"
That's all I heard as I teleported away.

SENSATION

Chapter 10

I popped into my apartment, in the bedroom. I really should have gone home, but - despite the hour - I had a sneaking suspicion my mother (and maybe Gramps, too) would be waiting up to hear how my date went. I didn't feel like talking to anyone right now. I flopped down on the bed and stretched out, mentally ticking off everything that had gone sideways tonight.

Movie: middling.

Date with pretty girl: disastrous.

Anonymity as Kid Sensation: blown completely to smithereens.

I was thinking that things couldn't get any worse when I heard voices. Coming from my living room.

I went invisible and my vision instantly switched over to infrared. I crept to the door and phased through.

I saw two people in the living room, male and female, standing almost side by side. The woman I immediately recognized as Esper. The male appeared as a huge mass of dark, swirling crimson. Alpha Prime.

This was obviously the op they were running. Somehow they had tracked me down. I thought I'd been careful but it's pretty clear that I was becoming lax in some way. I glanced around the room to see if anyone else was present. I didn't see anyone else, but something seemed...off. Then I saw it.

There were odd blotches on the wall and floor near where AP and Esper were standing. There were even some on the ceiling. I briefly wondered if this was some kind of mold or mildew festering almost under my nose.

104

SENSATION

"This is bad," Alpha Prime was saying. "A whole lot worse than just having an on-air brawl with the League."

"Agreed," Esper said. "I don't know that we have any choice here."

"Let's not jump to conclusions," said a third, unseen voice. Recognizing it as Mouse, I was a bit startled. How was he here in my apartment? Could he teleport, too? And where exactly was he? Then I remembered: holograms. I cycled my vision out of the infrared and through various wavelengths of light until I could see Mouse. He appeared as a pasty white, spectral presence between the dark gray humanoid forms of Esper and Alpha Prime.

"I'm not certain this would be jumping to conclusions," Esper stated. "I mean, look at this. I'm not sure I've ever seen anything like it. The type of person who could do this…"

Her voice trailed off, and for the first time I noticed that they were looking down at something near their feet. Something in the midst of all the splotches I had seen on the floor.

At first, I couldn't make it out. It looked like some three-dimensional rendering of Cubist art. There were jagged edges, sharp jutting angles, odd shapes…

Oh, no.

Almost involuntarily, I spun my vision through the light spectrum again until I came to something approaching normal. I didn't want to see it, but I had to. And I saw exactly what I expected.

The splotches on the wall weren't mold. It wasn't mildew on the ceiling. There wasn't any kind of infestation on my floor. It was blood. All of it. Blood. Everywhere. Blood. Everything. Blood.

And the body…it should be a crime to even conceive of doing something like this to another person. The culprit was deranged, had to be. And it was clear that no ordinary human had done this.

I felt an immense amount of sorrow for this person, whoever they were. I didn't know how they came to be in my apartment, but they didn't deserve to die like this. That's when I realized that the person's face had barely been touched. Even more, I recognized the victim. It was Pinchface. I sighed sadly and teleported to my house.

****

I popped into my bedroom at home. Just a few hours earlier, I had left practically on cloud nine about my date. I returned having been nearly electrocuted, "outed" as Kid Sensation, and probably wanted for murder. I couldn't imagine being more depressed.

I felt a questing probe from my grandfather. As I had suspected earlier, he and my mother had stayed up and were down in the kitchen, awaiting a full debriefing on my date. I clumped down the stairs heavily, my footsteps announcing my presence in a way that was atypical for me.

When I saw them sitting at the counter in the kitchen, I didn't have the heart to tell them the truth. So I made up a story about having a great date with Electra, but jointly deciding that we were better off as friends. They both offered me their sympathy and encouragement for whomever my next date might be with. Then, my mother went off to bed, leaving "her boys" to have a little man-talk. No sooner had her foot hit the stairs than my grandfather sent a stinging probe that jabbed me like a mental stick-pin.

<Now tell me what *really* happened.>

Rather than talk about it, I simply opened my mind and laid out the whole sordid mess. It took about fifteen seconds, after which he sat still, regarding me silently.

<Do you want me to make some calls? Sort this out?> he asked. <I'm still owed a few favors—>

<No! This is my problem; I'll handle it. I've been playing at hero as a bounty hunter and such. It's time I started acting like one. For real. You just figure out a time you can start giving me driving lessons.>

I suddenly got a feeling of warmth from him, an enveloping emotion of joy and smiling pride. It was the answer he'd wanted from me. He nodded and headed out the back door. I sighed, locked the door behind him, then headed up to bed.

SENSATION

INTERLUDE

Omen stood in front of an odd machine. That it was a complex and complicated device was evident, not so much because of its appearance - which was a curious mosaic of integrated circuitry, intricate components, and fused microelectronics - but because of its current state of being. It was semi-solid. Some parts could be touched and interacted with, while others were more ethereal.

Standing around Omen were the rest of his cohorts, all in person. Even Slate had dispensed with his golems and was here in the sickly yellow flesh.

"We stand on the precipice," Slate uttered with glee. "In very short order we shall be indomitable."

"Victory is not yet assured," Omen announced. "The Transdimensional Nanite Induction Platform is still fickle in some respects. We must still proceed with care."

"And let us not forget Kid Sensation," muttered Summit, who dwarfed his companions. "We have not yet closed the loop on him."

Omen smiled as he touched a dial on the device and colorful sparks began to fill the air and dance back and forth.

"Do not concern yourself with Kid Sensation," he stated with disinterest. "Our plans for dealing with him proceed unhindered."

SENSATION

Chapter 11

I awoke to the sound of someone trying to beat our front door down. Or at least that's what it sounded like. There was an incessant pounding on the door and ringing of the doorbell. I barely glanced at the clock - 5:13 a.m. - before anxiously teleporting downstairs. I reached out empathically for the person on the other side of the door, then yanked it open when I felt the cool familiarity of the visitor's emotions.

I opened the door expecting to see Braintrust. On the other side of the door was a tall, blonde woman in a red jogging suit. She had exquisite features and her hair was pulled back into a ponytail. She was accompanied by two men - practically twins - in dark t-shirts and sweatpants. I had never seen any of them before.

"Sorry to barge in unannounced like this, Jim," the woman said, "but we've got problems."

The voice was unfamiliar, but there was no mistaking the tone. It was BT. In fact, all three of these people were Braintrust clones.

<????> I felt a questing probe from my grandfather as the woman and her companions came in. I was about to open my mind and let him observe what was happening, when he relayed that BT clones were also at the door of his apartment. No need for a link now; the clones at his door would explain things to him, as these were hopefully about to explain to me.

"Jim?" I looked up and saw my mother on the stairs in her robe. "Is everything alright? Who are these people?"

Before I could respond, the female clone smiled at my mother and spoke. "Geneva, you're looking lovely, as always."

My mother frowned in thought for a moment, and then something like understanding dawned on her face.

"Braintrust," my mother said in a declaratory tone.

"In the flesh," said the blonde. "As usual, it's a pleasure to see you."

"Your compliments and flattery seem less sincere coming from a female clone," my mother stated with a grin. "What are you doing here?"

"You're in danger," the blonde said, all traces of humor vanishing. "I'll explain everything, but we have to leave now."

My mother looked at me. BT wasn't prone to exaggeration. If he said we were in danger then there was a real threat involved.

"Let's go," I said.

We marched outside to where BT had four cars waiting. As we were getting into the back seat of one of them - a spacious Towncar - two more male clones came around the corner of the house escorting my grandfather. Gramps got into the back seat with me and Mom. One of the male clones got in behind the wheel, while the blonde got into the front passenger seat. Each of the other three clones got into one of the other vehicles. We drove off with the other three cars following us.

It was still dark, at least another hour until dawn. There were cars parked on both sides of the street, forcing us to drive somewhat in the middle of the road. We'd gone about fifty yards when our driver pulled over and parked without warning before shutting the engine off. The other three cars kept going for about another ten yards, where they came to an intersection. The lead car went straight, while the other two went left and right, respectively.

I was about to ask what was going on when the blonde turned around and, looking out the back window, stated, "It's too late."

Following her lead, the three of us in the back seat turned and looked out of the back window as well. We were still close enough for our house to be visible, and that seemed to be the area where BT's gaze was focused.

At first, I didn't see anything. Except for what was chased away by streetlights, the darkness was all-encompassing. I cycled my vision through the light spectrum until I was able to see almost as well as in daylight. Mom, I knew, wouldn't have any issues with darkness. One of the things she had inherited from her mother was incredible night vision.

I was on the verge of telescoping my vision when I saw it. It came on like a shooting star initially, blazing a fiery path through the night. It arced through the sky and proceeded on a direct path towards our house, weaving a bright trail of flame behind it.

As it got closer, I could make out more minute details: a head...arms...legs. It was a super!

It was immediately obvious that the person was a female, but she was completely enveloped in flames. She stopped directly above our house, and - after waiting there for a few seconds - extended her hand out towards my grandfather's apartment. The garage was immediately ablaze.

Infuriated, I became insubstantial and began floating up through the roof of the car.

"No!" the blonde hissed. "Too dangerous!"

Too dangerous for me? BT must be referring to the fact that drawing attention might put Mom and Gramps in danger, since I had a number of powers I could use to avoid any injury. Regardless, I dropped back down into the car and became solid again.

At this point, the fire-woman was circling around the house, flames shooting from her outstretched hand and setting the entire structure ablaze. Then she zipped back and forth around the house in seemingly haphazard fashion.

"Any idea who that is?" I asked Braintrust.

"I believe she's called Incendia," came the response.

"What's she doing?" my mother asked as Incendia continued flying around the house erratically.

"Probably wondering why nobody's running out of the house screaming right about now," Braintrust replied.

Incendia circled around the house again, then zipped down the street in our direction. Everyone in the car ducked down as she flew past. I watched in silent fury, wishing our nullifier were reset and operational so I could pop her into it. Incendia stopped at the intersection, looked around desperately, then swished off to the left.

"Let's hope she's going after one of the bait cars," the blonde said as the driver started the engine and we drove off.

SENSATION

"Aren't you worried about your clones? That she'll kill them?" Mom asked.

Even Gramps chuckled at that one. "You must have forgotten: clones aren't essential elements of BT's makeup. They can look and act like the rest of us, but for him they're no more important than something like fingernails. For him, losing them is like getting a haircut."

"That's an oversimplification," the blonde said, "but true. Now, as to what this is all about: my mansion was attacked about an hour ago. All the clones there are a loss."

"I'm sorry–" I began.

"Don't be," the clone cut me off. "Your grandfather gave a good analogy. I'm basically unhurt."

"Did you recognize any of them?" I asked. Although the clones at the mansion were lost, anything they saw was preserved as part of BT's hive mind.

"A few, like Incendia," she responded. "But most were masked and wore body armor."

"How did they find you?" my grandfather chimed in.

"I'm not sure, but I have a theory." BT explained about Reilly Kubosh - Pinchface - and his power. "I believe he tracked down Kid Sensation, and through him, me. Or vice versa. But the most important thing isn't so much what they did but what they took."

The clone looked at me before going on. "The inhibitor."

I shrugged. "So what? We all know that the darn thing doesn't work half the time - only a quarter of the time, if you want the truth. And it has to be customized for a specific person. Unless they have someone specific in mind and a lot of info on the person's powers, it probably won't do them much good."

For one of the few times that I can remember, a Braintrust clone suddenly looked embarrassed. "You know," she said, "I don't care much for money, wealth, or power. It's all about information with me. Knowledge.

"I have designated clones whose only purpose, whose only job - only function - is to read newspapers. Others do nothing but read books. Some simply watch television, surf the internet, etc. I just want to know - *have* to know - everything."

This was stuff that I was already aware of, so I just nodded.

"That said, I'm afraid I haven't been entirely honest with you, Jim," the blonde continued. "In trying to perfect the inhibitor collar, I used data from the tests you let me conduct on you over the years to calibrate it. I used information concerning your biometrics and power set to fine-tune the device."

I really didn't like where this conversation was going, but if I didn't like it, my grandfather hated it.

"Are you crazy???!!!" my grandfather shouted at the clone. "You've been building an inhibitor to block my grandson's powers???!!!"

"No! Absolutely not!" she retorted. "It was never customized for him in any way. But Jim's probably the most versatile super on the planet. I had his data, so it was easy to use that information to help adjust the inhibitor for certain supervillains with powers similar to his."

If those words were meant to be soothing, they failed miserably. I could feel my grandfather's rage thundering across my brain. It was like a palpable force, a wind quickly and ferociously building up speed and pressure, ready to turn into a cyclone at any moment. And it wasn't even directed at me; it was pointedly focused on the blonde clone, who closed her eyes and began massaging her temples.

I've heard about how powerful my grandfather was in his heyday, how he could bring the strongest of villains to their knees with the power of his mind. I'd been told of how revered he was - even at his current age - among even the most dominant of psychics and telepaths. But I'd never felt his power brought to bear like this. The driver of the car started weaving, and I noticed blood coming out of his ears. I had to stop my grandfather before he accidentally flashburned someone's brain.

I slapped him, telepathically. Not hard enough to hurt him, but with enough force to get his attention, which was suddenly turned on me. Almost immediately, it felt like my head was going to explode. I winced, closing my eyes and groaning as, mentally, he came for me.

"Dad!" my mother screamed. And just like that, the pressure was gone. My mother's voice had cut through the red haze of his anger and brought my grandfather back to himself. It appeared that we were out of danger.

Even so, I had a stinging headache now. I cracked open my eyelids and saw my grandfather with a painful look on his face. His eyes were watery, as if he were about to cry, and I felt this terrible sadness coming from him as he realized what he had almost done.

<Next time, old man, you're going down.> Then I winked at him, which got me a smile in return.

"Now," I said, turning back to the clone, "back to the subject at hand. I can't say that I'm happy about what you did, but we don't have time to worry about that now. Plus, it doesn't sound like a big deal. They have an inhibitor, but it's customized for someone else. Big whoop."

"Normally, I'd agree with you," Braintrust countered, "but there's more. They didn't just take the collar. They also took your data from my PC. Separately, they don't add up to a lot, but in the hands of the right person - someone who knows what they're doing - they may be able to calibrate the inhibitor collar for you."

"Lovely," I said, leaning back. "So, now not only am I wanted for murder, but I've got to keep an eye out for persons unknown who may want to take away my super powers."

"What?!" Mom forcefully and incredulously interjected. "What murder?!"

It had slipped my mind that she didn't actually know what happened the night before, so I told the whole sordid story to her and BT. She frowned in severe disapproval when she learned about my apartment, but my grandfather assured her we could address that later.

"Interesting," said BT, staring off to the side in deep thought. "I think I have a theory about what's happening here. First, Jim, you find yourself being followed, so someone is definitely after you - especially when you consider the type of person they put on your tail. Then they take a device and information that can only be used specifically against you."

"I follow you," I said, "but I don't see your theory."

"Have you ever seen one of those documentaries, with predators like cheetahs hunting herds of antelopes and such in the wild?"

"Yeah," my grandfather commented. "The predator tries to get the herd moving, then isolate the weak - the old or the young - and bring them down. Are you saying that Jim is weak, and that's why they're after him?"

"No, quite the opposite," the blonde intoned. "I think they're after Jim because he's strong, and he's a threat to them somehow. But back to the predator theme, you'll notice that sometimes on those shows, if a weak member of the herd can't keep up, then the other members of the herd will sometimes form a circle around them, and just go around and around in large numbers so that the predator can't get to them without getting trampled.

"In this case, I think what they've tried to do is isolate Jim. He's only got a handful of people actively involved in his life: his mother, grandfather, and me. They take me out - or believe that they do - when they come for the inhibitor and Jim's data. Then they try to kill his mother and grandfather by burning down their house. Finally, by framing him for murder, they take away his ability to go to the authorities. In short, if they had succeeded at every step, Jim would have no one left to turn to and nowhere left to run. No family, no friends, no allies."

"Well, they may not be batting a thousand," Gramps said, "but they've been running up the score on us."

"Yeah," Mom said. "But there's got to be something we can do."

I'd been quietly thinking, and then something occurred to me.

"I think there's only one thing we can do," I said.

"What's that?" asked BT.

I grinned. "The unexpected."

SENSATION

Chapter 12

Two hours later, I walked into the Alpha League Headquarters and turned myself in. Of course, they were expecting me, seeing as how I had tipped them off regarding what I was planning to do.

Since there seemed to be a plan in motion to isolate me, the best recourse had seemed to be doing the opposite. That meant turning to the League for help rather than running away from them. Thus, after making sure that my mother and grandfather were safely stashed at another of Braintrust's hideouts (and after borrowing some clothes from BT), I had made the call to turn myself in.

I had initially wondered if they would assume it was a joke. After all, they probably got crank calls about Kid Sensation all the time. Yet, when I showed up, they were indeed expecting me. Or rather, Mouse was.

"Come with me," he said, not wasting time on small talk. He turned and marched down a hallway with me close behind.

"Where is everybody?" I asked.

"What, you thought you had a fan club?" he asked, stopping in front a door after a few twists and turns. "We didn't want you freaking out again, so I suggested that I talk with you one-on-one so it wouldn't feel like the whole League was ganging up on you. Again."

He smiled at that and opened the door, which led to a conference room. He took a seat in the first available chair and motioned for me to sit across from him.

"Besides," he continued, "we had some other emergencies that we had to respond to. Believe it or not, we actually spend a lot of time focused on things other than Kid Sensation - like saving the world."

I plopped down in the proffered seat. "So does this mean that I'm not under arrest?

"Arrest? For what?"

"The body in my apartment."

"Oh, so that *was* your apartment? Well, there was a little suspicion at first, but we established the time of death, and it just so happens that you were on a date with our own Electra then. So no, you're not under arrest."

I leaned forward as a great wave of relief washed over me. Whoever was after me, they hadn't expected that I would be doing anything social at the time of the murder, that I'd actually have an alibi. Tension that I didn't even know had been building evaporated almost instantly.

"So what now?" I asked.

"Well, continuing with my spiel from last night, we could really use someone like you. We're getting stretched pretty thin - so much so that we're even utilizing the super teens a lot more than we ever anticipated."

"You want me on the team?"

"Well, you passed the trials two years ago, using only one power from what we could tell, so you've earned a place here. Our issue has been finding you and getting you to accept."

He grinned, and I grinned back.

"There's something I need from you, though. And it's a bit of an emergency."

I quickly explained the situation regarding Braintrust, my mother, and my grandfather. Mouse took it all in without comment until I finished telling everything that had happened.

"Well, we can give your family some extra security, and I can fill in some of the blanks about what's happened," he said. "The guy we found in your apartment basically called us yesterday with info on Kid Sensation. He told us where to meet him, but was dead when we got there."

I explained our theory about framing me and he nodded sagely as I finished.

"I can't argue with the logic," he said. "But we can come back to that. Right now, let's go to my lab. There's some stuff I want to make you familiar with if you're going to be working with us now."

****

Mouse's lab was a complex affair with a lot of computers and machines and lots of data scrolling across several huge screens on the wall. It was located on the same subterranean level as the nullifier cells, but down a different hallway. Off to one side, I saw several bookcases stuffed to capacity with books. I also saw what appeared to be a refrigerator, and a small but ornate bathroom.

There weren't any Bunsen burners or colorful chemicals bubbling in test tubes, but the place still had kind of a mad scientist vibe. I was half-listening as Mouse was demonstrating some gadgets to me that would be part of my standard equipment when something in the corner caught my eye.

"What's that?" I asked, pointing at and walking towards an expensive-looking piece of equipment. It looked familiar to me, but I couldn't say from where exactly. I was reaching out to touch it when Mouse caught my wrist.

"You don't want to mess with this machine," he said. "It's a Transdimensional—"

"Nanite Induction Platform," I said in unison with him, grinning.

Mouse was suddenly alarmed. "How do you know that?"

"Know what?"

"The name of this machine. How do you know it?"

I shrugged. "I don't know. I guess I've seen one somewhere before."

"Uh-uh." Mouse shook his head vehemently. "You couldn't have. This is the only one in existence. So again, where did you see it?"

"Look, man, I don't know. Just around, I guess."

"That's not good enough," he said intensely. He was looking at me in a fierce and uncompromising way. "This is important, Kid. I need you to think back and tell me exactly when and where you saw this."

I sighed in exasperation. Then I told him about the dreams.

SENSATION

Chapter 13

We were back in the main conference room, where Mouse and I had previously had our little chat. Only this time, every chair in the room was filled with League members: Esper, Rune, Buzz, Feral, and a bunch of others. And, of course, Alpha Prime.

I looked around nervously. The last time I had been in a room with this many superheroes, I was in a fight. In fact, it was a fight with some of the very people in this room. I sincerely hoped that nobody held a grudge.

After I had told him my story, Mouse had convened an emergency meeting. Any Leaguer not currently on a mission or handling a crisis was to report in immediately. Within thirty minutes everyone available was present and accounted for. Mouse didn't waste any time on pleasantries; he asked me to recount what I'd told him.

"Basically, I've been having weird dreams - dreams about a group of supervillains trying to take over the world, destroy the League, and kill me. Mouse thinks my dreams are real."

I expected there to be some level of scoffing, some grunts of displeasure at being called in to an emergency meeting over foolishness. It was a sign of how much Mouse was respected and revered that no one said anything, although gazes did turn in his direction. Again, I wondered what kind of power he had that made the entire League treat anything he said as gospel.

Mouse gave the group a brief overview of the supervillains I had seen in my dreams. They were all heavy hitters and not to be taken lightly in any way, manner, or form.

SENSATION

"And before anybody asks," Mouse said, "the reason I believe his dreams are real is because he knows about things he couldn't have learned any other way. Frankly, I believe he has some kind of coeval cognizance that he uses in a subconscious manner to learn about things in the present or near-present."

"Is that true?" Esper asked me.

"I don't even know what that means," I said.

"*Pre*cognition is an ability that allows people to see the future," Mouse explained. "The one you dreamed about - Omen - takes his name from having that power. A person with a *post*-cognitive ability can see the past. What I'm calling coeval cognizance is kind of knowing about things in the present - or near the present - through some extrasensory means."

"But that's not a power that I've ever had!" I cried.

"Is it a power you could have developed?" asked Rune.

"No!" I shouted. "When I get a new power, I get this weird sensation..."

My words trailed off as I suddenly remembered. It was the buzzing sensation - the telltale sign of a new power - that had distracted me when Pinchface was following me. How long had I been having those dreams? I didn't know. It was then that I noticed that the room was abnormally quiet. Looking around, I saw that everyone was waiting for me to speak.

"On second thought, I recently had the sensation that I was developing a new power, but I didn't know what it was," I said. "It's possible it's this...cognitive ability."

"If I'm right," Mouse jumped in, "we're in danger. And by 'we', I mean the entire world."

Everyone was looking at Mouse, as he began explaining. "One of the things the Kid saw in his dream was a device that I'd made, the Transdimensional Nanite Induction Platform or TNIP. In short, it makes pocket dimensions - kind of like alternative worlds that you can enter, much like where we keep the Academy.

"However, the Academy exists in only one such dimension. This device creates hundreds, thousands of them. Maybe even millions. Moreover, you can move pieces of our world into them. Basically, you can carve the world as we know it up into a million different dimensional pieces."

Esper shrugged. "But what does that get you? What's the advantage of mincing the whole planet?"

"Ever hear the phrase 'divide and conquer'?" Mouse asked. "Imagine that you can trap a nation's navy in another dimension. Or that you can take away their army. Or their leadership."

Rune tapped his fingers on the table. "That would make the world a whole lot easier to take control of...or flat-out conquer."

"Listen, the things we're talking about, that's just the tip of the iceberg," Mouse stated. "There are a thousand worse things they could do with this technology."

Finally Alpha Prime stepped in. "So how do we stop them?"

Mouse smiled and turned towards me. "That's where the Kid comes in."

****

"You're insane," I said, not believing what I'd just heard. "You're certifiably insane."

"Probably," Mouse said, "but just hear me out anyway."

I shook my head in the negative. "I don't need to hear any more. I'm not doing it."

We were back in Mouse's lab. He had broken up the meeting and allowed me to glad-hand some people, but hadn't explained what his plan was for stopping the enemy until we got back to his lab.

"There's no other way," he replied.

"So, just to make sure I understand, you want me to teleport a team of superheroes to a place that I've only seen in my dreams?"

"That's about the gist of it."

"But that place may not even be real! I'm not sure I buy your cognizance theory. I might pop you all right out of existence. We've got no proof that this place is real!"

"I've got proof." I gave him a sideways glance as he continued. "When I'd turn on my machine, I'd get this weird reflective reading. I just assumed it was some kind of transdimensional echo. I didn't think it could be another device because mine was supposed to be the only one in existence. But it was actually the machines recognizing each other."

"Even if it's real, though, you want me to teleport you and a team to a place I've only seen in my dreams? Shouldn't you guys take a vote on this or something?"

He gave me an odd look and something new suddenly occurred to me. "Wait a minute," I said. "Is that why you didn't bring up the subject of this little mission in the conference room just now? You didn't think the rest of the League would agree to it, did you? You knew they'd vote you down!"

"On the contrary," he said, "I had no doubt that they'd agree with me. There wouldn't be a need for a vote. The reason I didn't mention it back there is because we have a mole."

I stood there in stunned silence. It felt like a full minute passed before I responded.

"What???!!" I said incredulously.

"These supervillains didn't just build a device identical to mine and then give it the same name by happenstance. Someone told them. Ergo, we have a mole in the League, and I didn't want to give them a hint of what we were up to."

"Even if that's true, I can't just go teleporting people to some place I've never been. And even if it works, have you thought about the fact that there are six major supervillains there? What if I land you dead smack in the middle of their hideout, and you have no idea of where you are or how to get out? Are you going to be prepared for something like that?"

Mouse scratched his chin in thought for a second, then looked at me with a sparkle in his eye.

"Okay," he said, "how about this: instead of transporting a team there, what about something small, like a bug?"

"Huh? You mean like a grasshopper?"

"No, not a *bug* bug; a mechanical bug - a listening device."

"Oh," I said in surprise. "Uh, sure, we can try that."

SENSATION

Mouse nodded, then stepped over to a nearby workbench. I saw him pull a miniature tool set out of a drawer on the workbench and go to work on a small object on the tabletop.

"Can this thing really do what you said?" I asked. "Create pocket dimensions - like where the Academy is?"

"That and worse," he answered as he worked, "although technically, the Academy actually exists in an alternate reality, one where sentient life never arose. Because of that fact, we use it for our own purposes. To be honest, though, the terms 'dimension' and 'alternate reality' are often used interchangeably - even by me, because it can make it easier to explain some things - but they're really two different concepts. In science, 'dimension' actually refers to—"

He glanced at me at this juncture, and something in my face must have indicated my low level of interest, because he gave a deep sigh and just said, "I guess it's not an important distinction, as long as people know what you mean." With that, he turned his attention back to the item on his workbench.

Five minutes later, he looked up, smiling.

"Voila!" he exclaimed, holding up his hand. In it he held a small circular object that looked like a black button set in a metal casing. He stepped over to the transdimensional platform and motioned for me to join him.

"You already know what this is," he said with a broad gesture at the machine. "If you'll look on this part of the device, you'll see a button that looks just like the bug here that I just cobbled together."

I looked where he was pointing and said, "Okay. I guess you want me to try to swap your bug for the real thing?"

"No, nothing so complicated. The bug is designed so that it looks like it belongs on the machine. Just put it right next to the real thing. Can you do that?"

I shrugged and took the bug from him. I stared at his machine one last time, then closed my eyes and tried to imagine it as I'd seen it in my dream. Buttons, screens, panels.... I concentrated, trying to recall the images and align the machine's design as it had appeared to me with Mouse's actual device. After a few seconds, I was able to picture it in unerring detail. I mentally looked for the button...there!

I felt the negligible weight of the bug vanish from my hand as I teleported it.

"Now, let's see if it worked," Mouse said, stepping over to a computer screen.

Looking over his shoulder, I saw what appeared to be a kind of radar.

"It's transmitting. Shouldn't be long before we get a fix."

"And then?"

"And then we go in, guns blazing."

SENSATION

Chapter 14

Mouse rounded up a group of superheroes for the planned assault in almost no time. Handpicked by Mouse as being above suspicion (i.e., none of them were the mole), they were secretly briefed and out the door in less than thirty minutes. Of course, they weren't going to let me - or any other teens - go along for the ride.

"You've done enough for now, Kid," Mouse had said. "With any luck, we'll have this thing wrapped up by the end of the day. Why don't you take a break for a few hours?"

With that, he had taken me to the teen lounge area. It was a smaller version of the break room at the Academy; there was a pool table, shuffleboard, and some other similar games, and a few flat-screen TVs on the walls. There were about ten teens in the room at the moment.

Mouse wasn't much for introductions. "Kid, this is everybody. Everybody, this is Kid Sensation."

Everything in the room came to a screeching halt, and a couple of people seemed to be waiting to hear a punchline. But Mouse was already gone, leaving me standing there looking like a lost sheep. When it appeared that this wasn't a joke, I found myself the center of a mad rush.

The other kids practically mobbed me, randomly shaking my hand and patting me on the back. It turns out that word of my little visit the night before was already circulating through the local grapevine. There were also a slew of rumors that I had to dispel (for example, that I had come back to challenge the League to another round).

SENSATION

After about fifteen minutes, a lot of the excitement died down. The mob gave me a bit more room to breathe, but I was still being peppered with questions. I also gave a short demonstration of a few of my powers, like teleporting around the room.

Someone asked to see my phasing ability, so I made a nearby card table insubstantial and pressed a pencil through the top of it. When I made the table solid again, the pencil was stuck in it. I left it there for a few moments, then phased the table again and pulled the pencil out.

"Why does the pencil punch through the table instead of getting cut in half?" a girl with glowing red eyes asked.

"Whatever I phase is the item that gets perforated," I answered. "Here, I made the table insubstantial, so the table is the item that gets punctured. But if I make the pencil insubstantial..." As I spoke, I phased the pencil, pushed it halfway through the table, then solidified it again. There was an audible clink as the bottom half of the pencil - which had been neatly sliced in two - fell and hit the floor under the table.

The girl with the red eyes reached down and picked up the piece of pencil off the floor. She seemed to be thinking about something, and then she asked, "Can you go the other way?"

"Huh?" I said, totally confused.

"The other way," she repeated. "Instead of becoming insubstantial, can you become more solid?"

"You mean like denser? Heavier?" I asked, frowning in thought. "I don't know. I've never tried it." In fact, the concept had never actually occurred to me, but it was certainly worth thinking about. I became so

131

focused on the idea that it was a few minutes before I fully joined the conversation again.

I was happy to see that Smokescreen, my erstwhile football teammate, was there. He had a camera and took a few pictures of me. A short time later, he asked, "After you shapeshift, how do you know how to go back to your own body? I mean, how do you keep from making yourself shorter, fatter, or something like that?"

I shrugged. "Instinct, I guess. I just know. I guess it's like a balloon that gets blown up, then has all the air let out of it; it just goes back to its original shape."

"Can you turn into someone right now? Like me?"

"I usually don't do people I know. I might base it on someone real, but I usually change something."

"Let's see!"

I tried to refuse, but after much cajoling, I shifted into Smokescreen. It only lasted about three seconds, but then everyone started clamoring for me to do someone else. I don't know why, but for some reason I decided to mimic Paramount.

"I'm Paramount," I said after changing shape. I struck a bodybuilding pose. "I'm the most gorgeous hunk of super teen you'll ever see. I'm strong, and pretty, and fast, and pretty, and...did I say pretty?"

Everyone was rolling with laughter as I continued my impersonation. Without warning, however, a deafening silence settled over the room. I was in the middle of mimicking Paramount when I turned to see what had happened - and there was the real Paramount standing in the doorway.

SENSATION

I casually changed back to myself and flopped down on a nearby stool. Paramount entered the room, making a beeline for me. The path between us cleared as students quickly stepped aside for him, like townspeople in a spaghetti Western getting out of the way of a gunfight. He strolled right over to where I sat and just stopped. He stood there for about thirty seconds just looking me over, up and down, as if I were a fish he had hooked and was deciding whether to keep.

"So, it's true," he said finally. "They found you."

"I was never lost," I replied.

"Well then, you decided to come out of hiding," he sneered.

I really wasn't in the mood and I contemplated just getting out of there, but I didn't want to even imply that I was intimidated by him.

"Call it whatever makes you feel better," I said. "It doesn't make a difference to me. Whatever you say."

"That's right," he said, tapping himself in the chest with a thumb. "Whatever *I* say. And as long as we have that understanding, welcome to the team."

He extended a hand, which I looked at for a second in surprise before taking. As expected, he squeezed unnecessarily hard.

"Just so you know," he whispered, leaning in close, "in a one-on-one fight, I'd take you in a second."

He let go, almost throwing my hand away, and turned towards the door. He'd gone about three steps when he stopped and looked back as if he'd forgotten something.

"One other thing," he snarled venomously. "Don't ever do me again."

SENSATION

Of course, after Paramount left the room, I immediately shifted into him, much to the amusement of the other kids.

****

Needless to say, Paramount's appearance put a damper on things in the break room. I still hadn't really seen the facilities, so a group of the other teens offered to show me around. I thought about the last purported tour I was invited on and almost declined. I'm glad I didn't.

They first took me to the weight room. It was singularly impressive. I'd never seen multi-ton weights before (outside of pictures). Likewise, there were treadmills that could go at hundreds of miles per hour. (I even tried one out.) There was also a massive training room that simulated attacks from supervillains via holograms.

All in all, it was great. The only downside was that, on one little trip from one place to another, we passed Electra in the hallway. She stopped when she saw me, and made a gesture for me to approach.

"Look, I'm sorry about last night," she said.

"What's to be sorry about?" I said blandly. "You guys had been looking for Kid Sensation; you found him. You just had to play with my emotions to do it."

"Jim, I wasn't trying to—"

"I don't know what you were trying to do and right now I don't care. I liked you, and you used that to trick me and lead me on."

"I wasn't leading you on. I liked you, too. But I also have a duty to the League! You'll learn that after you've been here for a while."

SENSATION

I walked away without saying anything. She did have a point, but I wasn't ready to admit it. She could stand to stew in her own juices for a little while.

SENSATION

Chapter 15

It was late afternoon when someone brought back word that the team had returned. (Apparently the secret mission had only remained "secret" for a limited amount of time.) We'd finished the tour quite a while earlier, and I was actually in the League cafeteria eating a sandwich.

All of the kids kind of scattered, running off to try to get news of how the mission had gone. According to the rumor mill, it was a success, but I was hoping to get more detail. I tried to be patient and give them time to debrief, but after about thirty minutes I couldn't take it anymore. I started asking random people where I could find Mouse. Eventually, someone told me that he was probably in his lab. I didn't have the clearance to physically get through all the checkpoints, so I just teleported there instead.

I appeared right in front of Mouse, who was busy typing something in on a computer tablet. I've teleported in front of people before and most of them find it startling; Mouse barely looked up.

"It's been less than a day," he said, "and I can already tell that we're going to have to put a bell on you."

"I need to know what happened," I said anxiously. "Remember, my family is in danger."

"It's something of a mixed report," he said, finally looking up.

"What do you mean?"

Mouse gave me a quick overview of what had happened. The bug he'd had me plant was also a homing beacon that had given them a location that turned out to be deep underground. Despite Mouse's earlier statement about going in "guns blazing," the team had actually tried

136

to be as stealthy as possible. But, as usually happens, they were eventually revealed and that's when the real fight started.

"One of those villains tried to use the TNIP," Mouse said. "I assume they were going to try to trap the team in a pocket dimension. So I blew up the machine."

"You blew it up?" I was incredulous. "How?"

"With the bug you planted. It was actually a Triple-B device: bug, beacon…and bomb."

"Wait," I said. "You had me teleport a bomb somewhere? And you didn't tell me???!!!"

"Look, Kid," he said in an explanatory tone. "I didn't know how much time we had or what exactly they were planning to do. I just knew we had to stop them, and that meant preventing them from using that device – by any means necessary. So yes, I had you teleport a bomb, and I didn't tell you because I didn't have time to deal with it if you were some kind of conscientious objector who got squeamish at the thought of people getting hurt."

I didn't know how to respond. I was overflowing with an emotion that I couldn't put a name to: fury and disbelief bundled with remorse and finality. I understood what Mouse was saying, but I'd never used my powers in a way that might kill someone. It's not that I couldn't accept it – Gramps had instilled in me the fact that death was sometimes unavoidable in order to achieve the greater good – but it was something you usually had an opportunity to make your peace with beforehand, if only for a few seconds.

I let out a long breath that I didn't know I'd been holding.

"How many?" I asked.

"How many what?"

"How many died? From the bomb I planted?"

"Oh, none from what we can tell."

My relief was almost palpable and certainly visible, because Mouse started grinning.

"Is that why you were suddenly so uptight? You thought you'd killed somebody?"

"I didn't know..."

"Maybe I should finish this story, then. The bomb went off, but it was a shaped charge, only meant to destroy the machine. Unfortunately, it wasn't strong enough; the device was only damaged initially."

"So it's still functional?"

"No. The bomb didn't immediately destroy it, but it became seriously destabilized. The technology underlying it became corrupt, and it began creating random proximal pocket dimensions."

"What does that mean?"

"As best as I can tell, all six of our supervillains are trapped in a pocket dimension of their own creation."

****

It was a little more complicated than the way Mouse explained it. He'd had to reverse-engineer the sequence of events following the detonation of his bug-bomb to find out what happened. The villains in charge had indeed been seemingly trapped in one of the pocket dimensions. However, the machine had created thousands of such pockets before it permanently ceased functioning. Moreover, there was no way to identify or track the specific pocket the villains were in. In short, they were trapped to a certain extent, but at the same time not in custody.

On the flip side, the raid had resulted in the actual capture of a number of henchmen, both normal and super. Those that were normal had been handed off to the authorities. Those with superhuman abilities were being held in the League's nullifier cells until proper transportation could be arranged. I offered to teleport them, but Mouse declined.

"It's not really a transport problem," he said. "It's a space-available problem. See, we have special prisons built to hold super criminals, but we can't send them to prison without a trial. It's still a free country, after all. However, we can hold them until they're actually tried - assuming they don't make bail. Right now, all the jail cells are at their legal limit, so we'll keep some of them here until a slot opens up, bail is set, or what have you."

That seemed reasonable, and I probably wouldn't have given the situation much more thought under other circumstances. However, he ran through a list of names of those who had been captured, one of which made my ears perk up: Incendia.

I immediately teleported to the room with the nullifier cells. The room already had a good number of occupants, both teen supers and League members. My appearance startled a couple of kids, but they recovered quickly enough to answer my questions. Apparently Incendia was being held in the third cell. I walked down, eager to get a closer look at the person who had burned my house to the ground.

I was a little shocked when I finally saw her. She was just a teenager, probably the same age as me. And, when not encased in living flame, it seemed that she had pale skin, cold blue eyes, and curly blond hair. She gave me an icy glare that would have frozen an ocean. It was as if she knew me, and to be frank, there was something about her that was oddly familiar. Yet, I had never seen her before earlier that day, when she had treated my home like a place to make s'mores. (Had it only been that morning? It seemed like a lot longer – weeks at least.)

My reverie was interrupted by a flash going off next to me. It was Smokescreen, taking pictures as usual.

"Is that allowed down here?" I asked, nodding towards his camera.

"Oh, sure," he replied. "The League likes to have all this stuff documented. There are actually hidden video cameras in the room, but I talked them into letting me take some still shots. Officially, all the pictures I develop belong to the League, but it's just a hobby for me – no commercial gain involved – so I don't care."

"You said 'develop'?" I noted curiously.

"Yeah, I'm old school," he said with a grin. "My dad was a photographer and he taught me."

"Tainted you is more like it," said a new voice, Aqua, who I hadn't noticed. "You really should try digital."

"Nah," Smokescreen said. "I like getting my hands dirty – I've got a darkroom and everything in my quarters. It makes me feel like I'm close to my old man."

I gave him a pat on the shoulder in understanding fashion. I gave a fleeting thought as to whether I'd ever be close to my own father, then dismissed the notion. When I was a kid, I used to dream about my father showing up one day and proclaiming me as his own to the world, like the Wizard of Oz stepping out from behind the curtain. I had put that dream far out of my mind years ago, and it was best to keep it that way.

I watched as Smokescreen snapped a picture of Aqua in front of Incendia's cell, then began to make my way out.

SENSATION

Chapter 16

Following my departure from the nullifier cells, I teleported to the safe house where Braintrust was keeping my family. I was pleased to see that Mom and Gramps were fine, and well-protected by a large number of BT clones. (After learning about Mouse's suspicions of a mole, I passed on his offer of League security.)

I brought them up to speed on what had happened. There was relief that Incendia had been captured, but it was decided that they should continue to lie low for a couple of days. After spending a few hours with them – including having dinner – I said my goodbyes and popped back to the League.

In an ideal world, had my original Teen Super Trial not become a PR disaster, I would have been given living quarters at Alpha League HQ like the other super teens being sponsored. Of course, teen quarters generally saw limited use. During the school year, teen supers were in residence at the Academy; during the summer, most spent some time at home with family.

There were, however, a few times during the summer when it was mandatory that super teens stay at their team HQ. This was one of those times. (The general understanding was that staying with a superhero team the last few weeks of the summer got a super teen back into the right frame of mind – as well as physical shape – before heading back to the Academy.) Thus, the League's teen population was impressive in size at present.

That being the case, I was pleasantly surprised that they were still able to provide me with a room. It turns out, though, that I needn't have worried. There were far more rooms than the League would probably ever utilize. I was placed on one of the floors for males, next door to Smokescreen – presumably a friendly face in case I had any questions.

My room was fairly spacious, about the equivalent of a one-bedroom apartment. There was a quaint living area, a kitchenette, and a nice-sized bedroom with an ample closet. Someone had even gone to the trouble of placing clothes in the closet that were my size.

It was dark when I got back, though not necessarily late. Still, it had been a long day, so I took a leisurely shower, thinking about everything that had happened. The shower was an edgeless, clear-glass model with a handle that doubled as a towel rack on the outside. The hot water felt good against my skin, almost like a soothing massage, kneading out tension that I didn't know I had.

When I was finished, I turned off the shower and then phased, becoming insubstantial. Water that had clung snugly to my body a second before cascaded down to the floor of the shower. Having dispensed with the need for a towel, I pulled on a pair of boxers and a t-shirt.

The bathroom sink was a single vanity set in the center of a countertop about five feet long, with a mirror of equal length set in the wall. The mirror was fogged from my use of the shower, so apparently I would need the towel after all. I turned and pulled it from the handle of the shower door, and when I looked back to the mirror I almost jumped out of my skin.

Aqua was sitting over the sink, feet dangling off the edge of the counter. She was wearing a robe that had hung on the back of the bathroom door a second ago. She laughed at the look of surprise on my face.

"Serves you right," she said between giggles. "Now you know what it feels like when you pop up on people out of nowhere."

"How...how'd you get in here?" I asked, trying to recover.

She tapped the sink. "Any place that water can go is accessible to me." Then she turned to water – clear, animated liquid in brash female form – then she reverted back.

"How long have you been in here?" I asked.

She smiled, putting her arms around my neck and leaning in close. "Let's just say that I'm a little harder to shake off than that water in the shower."

Blushing, I leaned away from her, pulling her hands from around my neck at the same time.

"Not to be rude," I said, "but what are you doing here?"

"Just checking to see how you're settling in," she said, pouting a little. "So, how's everything so far?"

"Fine. I've got no complaints. The room's comfortable, and almost everybody's been pretty nice."

"So, what's it like having all that power?" she asked, abruptly changing the subject.

"What do you mean?"

"I mean, you're probably one of the most powerful supers on the planet. You took down the whole Alpha League by yourself a few years ago."

I shook my head. "I didn't really take anyone down. We just kind of butted heads, and everybody went away licking their wounds. The problem was that it was all caught on film and ended up being an embarrassment for everyone – me included."

SENSATION

"What did you have to be embarrassed about? With power like yours, you could make almost any super on the planet bow down to you — and make normal people worship you like a god."

I frowned. "That wouldn't be right."

"Sometimes might makes right," she said, smiling.

I was so focused on what she was saying that I didn't realize that she was leaning towards me again until her lips brushed mine. There was a jolt, an emotional charge that shot through me, along with a thousand conflicting emotions. On some level, I knew instinctively that Aqua was leading me down a dark path, that she was manipulating me. I should have drawn away, but instead, when she pressed for a deeper kiss, I kissed her back.

Her arms were around my neck and I pulled her close. In my brain, I felt a small spark igniting, a tiny plume of flame quickly fanning into a wildfire crackling across my mind.

This is wrong! Wrong! WRONG!

Finally, I pulled back, held her at arm's length.

"Don't you have a boyfriend?" I asked. "Herc?"

"Please," she said dismissively. "He's a mobile slab of rock. I've known amoebas with more brain cells. Getting him to have an original thought is like trying to nail Jell-o to a tree.

"Besides," she continued, trying to close the distance between us, "you didn't seem to have a problem with it a minute ago."

I took a step back. "Well, I came to my senses."

Her eyes suddenly narrowed. "This isn't about Herc. It's about Little Miss Live Wire. Electra. You really like her."

I didn't say anything.

"Interesting," she said, staring at me as if some new thought had struck her out of the blue. "Anyway, just think about what I said."

"What part?"

"All of it," she said with a wink. Then her body became liquefied and arced towards the sink as if from a spout. The robe dropped to the floor, empty.

SENSATION

Chapter 17

I lay in bed for a while after Aqua left, trying to go to sleep. I was worn out, but sleep wouldn't come. Something about my conversation with her kept nagging at me. After about an hour, I gave up on getting any sleep and tossed on a pair of cargo pants and a polo shirt. I phased, then flew outside the window and up to the roof.

Sometimes, when I can't sleep, I like to gaze up at the stars. Maybe it's the fact that part of my heritage is alien, or maybe it's just knowing that I've got family out there, but being up in the air and looking at the nighttime sky just seems to put me at ease. There's something about the vastness of space, the immensity of it, that makes any problem you have pale in comparison.

The roof of Alpha League's HQ was actually a multi-level affair that served a couple of purposes. There was a recreational area that consisted of a pool and a couple of cabanas. On the more functional side (which actually sat about two stories higher), there was a utility shed, a retractable dome that housed a helicopter landing pad, and a few more structures whose use I wasn't sure of.

I was so lost in my own thoughts that I didn't see him at first. I had actually thought I was alone. The first inkling I had of anyone else being around was the slight ripple of his cape in the nighttime breeze. I was floating on the recreational side of the building at the time, and the sound – coming from above me – made me look up to the helipad area. I couldn't actually see him at that point, just the end of his cape fluttering.

SENSATION

I flew up and peeked over the edge. It was *him*. He was just floating there, looking up at the sky as I had been a few moments ago. His back was to me, but I'd known who it was before I looked: Alpha Prime.

I turned away, ready to fly back down when I heard him call out.

"It's okay," he said, glancing back at me. "You don't have to leave."

I hadn't even realized he knew I was there. I seesawed back and forth in my mind for a second, then came to a decision. I flew over next to him.

"Sorry," I said. "I didn't realize anyone else was up here. I just...the stars just help me clear my head."

He smiled and nodded. "I know the feeling."

We floated in silence for a few minutes, right next to each other but at the same time in our own separate worlds. I was probably in one of the most enviable positions on the planet. Most kids dream about getting to meet the world's greatest superhero, and at one time I had been just like them - but I had grown up since then. Still, after a while, I couldn't help but wonder what he was thinking and feeling. Gently, I reached out empathically.

He was a swirl of emotions: pride, satisfaction, contentment, and a sense of purpose. However, there was only measured happiness and limited joy, and underpinning it all was a sadness and longing so deep and aching that it was tangible.

Maybe he felt my probe, because suddenly he spoke.

"I'm not from here, you know," he said, as if revealing some great secret. "This world."

SENSATION

I nodded, saying nothing. Everyone knew his story, but it seemed important to let him tell it.

"I certainly never should have ended up here, or ended up as what I am. Back where I came from, I wasn't anybody important." He laughed. "I wasn't even important enough to be a nobody."

"My brother and I, we were janitors," he went on. "We were part of the nighttime cleaning crew at an advanced research lab. One night, we're cleaning up, and we notice that one of the doors that should have been locked - and off-limits - wasn't.

"At the time, the rule was to clean any and every room that we had access to. That being the case, we went in. Long story short, they were experimenting with some kind of interdimensional device and my idiotic brother accidentally turned it on. It landed us here."

I ventured to ask a question. "So, if you were a nobody on your own world, does that mean that most people there are more powerful than you?"

"They wish," he said, laughing out loud. "No, people on my world don't have powers. It's a rather humdrum existence compared to what goes on in this place."

"How did you get your powers then?"

He shrugged. "No one really seems to know, but the prevailing theory among most scientists is that it happened when we made the trip over. It only seemed like a second to us, but it's possible we were in some kind of interdimensional void for a lot longer. Moreover, there are a lot of forces in those regions that nobody understands. Long story short, I was probably exposed to something there which gave me my powers.

SENSATION

"Furthermore, some of that force or energy seems to have leaked into this world with us, because the advent of supers on this planet coincided with our arrival. Nobody had super powers prior to that. Hell, I was actually here a decade before I figured out that I had any."

"What about your brother?" I asked.

I must have hit upon an uncomfortable subject, because suddenly his face soured.

"He's still around, but we're estranged at the moment." He looked wistful for a second. "Most people don't even know that I have a brother. They know my story, but not many know that I didn't come here alone. But that crisis we had today — dealing with that interdimensional headache — it kind of brought everything back. Every now and then one of the missions will do that to me, and when it does, I come up here.

"According to the scientists, what I described as another dimension - my home dimension - is technically the same world, just a different reality. One where history somehow deviated from the past as known here. I can't see alternate realities, though, so I like to look at the sky sometimes and assume my world is out there."

I didn't say anything, so I think he probably took my silence for boredom. (In actuality, I was reflecting back on Mouse's brief lecture on dimensions earlier and wishing I'd paid more attention.)

"Anyway," he said, "I'm sure you've got better things to do than listen to me reminisce. What about you; what's your family like?"

It was a question that I, naturally, wanted to avoid. So I sidestepped it, giving vague responses about living with my mother and grandfather.

"And what about your dad?" he asked.

I shrugged and tried to look unfazed, but the question was like a punch in the gut. "He's never really been around." Then I looked him in the eye. "In fact, I don't think he'd recognize me if I were standing right in front of him."

He nodded sagely, but didn't say anything. I turned and started to leave, but I'd barely moved before he spoke again.

"Hey, Kid," he said, almost as an afterthought. "I don't know if anyone's done it yet, but on behalf of the entire Alpha League I want to apologize to you for what happened two years ago. Things never should have gotten out of hand like that."

I looked at him and tried to speak but nothing would come out. It's as if there were some kind of short-circuit between my brain and my mouth. I felt my eyes suddenly becoming irritated in a maddening way, so I nodded once and then teleported to my room.

SENSATION

Chapter 18

I had thought I'd felt tears coming on when I left the roof, but that didn't happen. Nevertheless, my eyes still felt a little odd, so I left my room and went next door to ask Smokescreen if he had any eyedrops. He answered on the first knock.

"Hey, man," he said. "Come on in."

I found myself entering a dimly lit apartment that, for all intents and purposes, appeared to be a duplicate of my own.

After learning what I needed, Smokescreen disappeared and came back a few minutes later with a small bottle of eyedrops.

"Here you go," he said. "Sorry about the lack of lights, but I'm in the middle of developing."

"No problem. Thanks for the drops."

"Hey!" he said with sudden enthusiasm. "Would you like to see them?"

In all honesty, I didn't. It had been a long and tiresome day, and I really just wanted a chance to recharge my batteries. However, he was a nice guy and was probably my only friend here at the moment.

"Sure," I lied as I put a few drops in my eyes.

I followed him into his bedroom and then into his closet, where he had his darkroom set up. It appeared to be a little more spacious than mine, but I didn't know if that was because it actually was larger or because he'd moved all articles of clothing out of it.

The room was aptly named, because the only light came from some type of low-wattage, red bulb that Smokescreen called a "safelight." I admittedly didn't know very much about film developing (apparently it's a dying art in the digital age), but Smokey – as he liked to be called – did a great job of explaining everything and actually making it sound interesting. Before long, he had me engrossed in the entire process, from the importance of cleaning your development tank to presoaking your film.

Initially, it was a struggle not to switch my vision over to infrared or one of the other light spectrums. It would certainly have made it a lot easier to see everything. However, I'd learned long ago that the best way to understand some things was to experience them, so I kept my eyesight normal.

After a quick overview of how everything worked, he showed me some of his finished products. I had to admit that Smokey was either a pretty good photographer or a pretty good developer; some of the finished photos that he let me see were world-class, in my opinion.

"What's this?" I asked, indicating a film negative that he had sitting to the side. The reddish-brown piece of film showed two faces. Like most images of people on negatives, both visages were void of pigmentation, but you could still make out certain details. There was a girl in the foreground, but then – immediately over the girl's right shoulder and a little farther back – another girl. Both faces appeared to be identical.

Smokey glanced at it before responding. "Oh yeah, this is the picture I took of Aqua in front of the nullifier cell with the girl who was captured. I'm not sure what's going on. It looks like Aqua's face maybe got superimposed on this other girl–"

"Incendia," I interjected.

SENSATION

"Yeah, that's her: Incendia," he said. "Anyway, I was going to look at it later. Maybe it's some kind of double-negative, or the film got damaged. Who knows?"

I was only half paying attention to him at this point. My mind was racing, trying to form a coherent gestalt from bits and pieces of scattered information at my disposal.

When it finally hit me, I realized that I had practically been in a trance, and Smokey was snapping his fingers in front of my face.

I turned to him and said, "It's not a double-negative."

SENSATION

Chapter 19

We let Mouse into Smokey's quarters, now with all the lights on, almost immediately after he knocked. He came in without waiting for an invite as soon as the door opened.

"Jeez, Kid," he said, looking at me, "you ought to come with a warning label. Almost every emergency call I've had in the past twenty-four hours has related to you in some way." He flopped down on Smokey's couch, slightly irritated. "Now what's this all about?"

He was wearing the same clothes as earlier, so it looked like he hadn't been to bed yet. Tracking him down had been fairly easy. Every teen super is given a mentor to work with. When I'd told Smokey that I needed to reach Mouse, he'd called his mentor, Feral, who had then relayed the message. We'd stressed that it was an emergency, but were told that Mouse would come by Smokey's room as soon as possible. It had actually taken just a little over fifteen minutes, and Smokey had used the intervening time to set up a demonstration on his computer.

I broke the ice with the simple truth. "I think Aqua's your mole."

All trace of annoyance vanished as he responded. "I'm listening."

Smokey flopped down next to Mouse with his laptop as I began by conveying Aqua's comments from the diner during our triple date. "She mentioned that she had a twin sister. An *identical* twin sister."

Mouse shrugged. "So? There's nothing special about that."

"Except that her twin sister is Incendia, who you're currently holding in a nullifier cell downstairs."

"Is this a joke? I've seen her; they look nothing alike."

"That's where you're wrong." I passed him the negative. "They look exactly alike. Identical."

"I can see a resemblance–" he began.

I quickly cut him off, turning to Smokey and saying, "Show him."

Smokey had scanned the negative images into his laptop. Now he enhanced the size of Incendia's visage and overlayed it on top of Aqua's face while Mouse watched. It was a perfect match.

"Nobody would ever think of them as twins, because one's White and the other's Black, but take away pigmentation and their features match. They're identical."

Mouse seemed to be absorbing this, so I went on. "Plus, their abilities are diametrically opposed – fire and water – like a lot of super-powered twins." It was true; twins with powers often had conflicting abilities, like being able to control warmth and cold.

"Okay, there's some merit to what you're saying," Mouse admitted, "but it still doesn't quite add up. For instance, I've never taken the transdimensional platform out of my lab, and she's never been allowed in unsupervised; when would she have seen it? Moreover, the TNIP is a complex piece of machinery to say the least. The schematics, design, and data for it changed almost daily when I was building it. For them to keep up with its construction and stay on pace the way they did, she'd have had to send them updates constantly, and we would have noticed that volume of communication. So how or when could she have told anyone about it?"

"You do know that Aqua can take on liquid form?" I asked.

"Yes, I think we've all seen it."

"Well, she popped up in my room tonight – came through the sink. Said she can go anywhere water does." As Mouse took a second to absorb this, I went on. "Now, are you trying to tell me that you don't have a single source of water in your lab? No water line to the refrigerator? No sink in the bathroom? No toilet? Getting in to see it would be a piece of cake for her."

With respect to communications, I vaguely referenced a friend who consisted of clones sharing a hive mind.

"Wait," said Smokey, speaking for the first time since Mouse arrived. "Are you saying she might be a clone like that? With a hive mind?"

I shook my head. "I don't think so. When we were eating dinner, Aqua mentioned that she and her sister don't speak; then she laughed, saying it was a private joke. I took it to mean that maybe she and her sister were estranged. But now I think that what she actually meant is that she and her sister don't *have* to speak to each other. Each already knows what the other knows."

Smokey frowned, but Mouse picked up on the idea, saying, "That might actually make sense. Think about it. Identical twins actually start out being the same person. They form from a single egg that splits. Maybe this is an instance where they split into separate people physically, but their minds remained joined."

"So what are we talking about here – telepathy?" Smokey asked.

"No," I said, shaking my head. "Not telepathy. Each just automatically knows what the other is thinking, feeling, doing, and so on."

"Now, just to sum up your theory," Mouse said, "you think Aqua's the mole. She's basically used the water pipes to have free rein of the building, including sneaking into my lab. This joint consciousness she has with her twin allowed her to communicate information about the TNIP to her sister — and thereby to numerous supervillains — such that they could build their own transdimensional device. Sound good so far?"

I nodded, and he continued. "So that just leaves one question: why haven't they attacked?"

"What do you mean?" Smokey asked.

"Well," Mouse went on, "if they've already compromised Aqua — and who knows how many others — they've got a lot of our passwords, entry codes, etc. Why haven't they stormed this place?"

I thought about it for a few seconds before responding. "Maybe there's nobody to give the order."

They both looked at me, puzzled, so I explained. "Right now, their leaders are trapped in a pocket dimension. Prior to that happening, there was no need to attack this place; they could have had a bloodless coup by trapping the entire League in the same type of pocket dimension."

"So we missed being the site of a pitched battle by default?" Mouse asked, chuckling.

Smokey, however, seemed less sure. "But what if those guys in the other dimension get out? They could decide to attack then, right?"

SENSATION

"But they can't get out," Mouse said. "They'd need another transdimensional device, and the only other one is—"

He stopped, and we stared at each other, frozen by the thought that had occurred to both of us simultaneously. Then a wicked series of explosions rocked the entire building.

Chapter 20

It was a well-coordinated attack, more so – as we would find out later – because it came from an internal rather than an external source. That said, even a poorly executed attack would probably have been successful. We were just too slow in coming to our conclusion about an assault being imminent.

My gut reaction was actually to teleport myself, Mouse, and Smokey to Mouse's lab. That's where the TNIP was and that's what logic indicated our attackers were after. However, Mouse stopped me; instead, he directed me to teleport everybody I could find to safety outside.

I did so, starting with him and Smokey. Needless to say, it was the right course of action. I was somewhat ashamed; my power had the ability to save lives, but my first thought had been to get into a fight. (Or rather, to choose a stance – protecting the TNIP – that would get me into one.) Thankfully, Mouse still had his head on straight. Thus, per his instructions, I ran from floor to floor at top speed, teleporting everyone I could find outside.

There were a few other explosions as I continued my rescue attempts. One of them was accompanied by a mental shriek – a banshee wailing across the surface of my mind with concussive force. Everyone felt it at some level, but probably only a few recognized it for what it was: Esper dying, or so close to death that it didn't matter.

Like me, others used their talents to try to locate or help victims. Buzz zipped through the building even faster than I did, racing individuals out one at a time. A flyer that I didn't recognize rescued people who were trapped in places that were difficult to reach.

Mouse, meanwhile, tapped like a madman on his computer tablet. You would have thought he was saving the world, as focused as he was. In fact, he never even took time to check on any of the injured.

It was several hours before we were sure we'd gotten everyone we could out and stabilized as much of the building as possible. There was lots of bad news.

Feral had almost every bone broken and was in a coma. Power Piston was standing too close to a blast zone and was out of commission for at least a month. A group of teens in the lounge area had suffered from smoke inhalation and minor burns.

To the extent that a silver lining existed, we were lucky that Feral had a powerful metabolism and was expected to recover. Also, Esper was not dead; Rune had come floating up out of the rubble with her body in an ethereal bubble (although, as Smokey commented, she initially looked like a charred corpse). Like Power Piston, she had been caught in the immediate blast radius of an explosive device, but Rune's magic was sustaining her and would keep her alive.

All in all, a good number of League members were down for the count. Oddly enough, though, the invulnerable member of the League, Alpha Prime, was nowhere to be found.

There was much speculation about what exactly had happened. Mouse had asked me to say nothing until he revealed the results of his escapades on his computer tablet: digital transmission of the security footage from League HQ.

SENSATION

Aside from the three of us who had been in Smokey's room, the evidence on the camera probably came as a surprise to all other members of the League. Our own people had attacked us: a group of super teens.

It wasn't just any assembly of teens, though. It was primarily the tight little clique that made up Paramount's thuggish entourage. However, it included not only a bunch of heavies like Goon and Herc, who were generally considered the next generation of super-strong brawlers, but also a number of others with unique talents, like Aqua. All in all, it was a deadly cartel that you wouldn't want to meet in a dark alley.

Led by Paramount, they had first gone to the nullifier cells to free the prisoners. Feral had been on duty; although they had caught him off-guard, he gave as good as he got for a few minutes, but even his preternatural strength and stamina couldn't hold out against so many forever. Eventually he'd fallen, but they had kept pounding and stomping him wickedly until his entire body seemed pulped.

Next, they'd gone to Mouse's lab. Aqua apparently went to liquid form and gained entry via the pipes, then opened the door from the inside. A few minutes later, Alpha Prime came floating in, called down by Paramount per the audio. While he was talking to his son, Aqua used the TNIP to trap him in a pocket dimension.

It was an odd thing to watch. First there was just Alpha Prime talking to Paramount. Then an unusual glow formed around him, in the shape of a sphere. It came into existence and encased him so quickly that there

162

was no time to react. Alpha Prime beat against the bubble holding him, but to no effect. Then it began to fade, disappear. Paramount laughed as his father appeared to wink out of existence.

****

"At least we know what happened to him," said Buzz as we watched the footage.

We were currently in one of the League's auxiliary facilities (a safe house of sorts), one hopefully off the grid in terms of what Paramount's crew knew about. They had mechanized medical facilities here, so those who were injured were able to receive treatment. The rest of us had turned our attention to the security footage.

After trapping Alpha Prime, Paramount had lifted the TNIP en masse and carried it to the garage, where a van waited. He'd loaded it up and driven off with about half of his crew while the rest of them planted bombs. In the resulting confusion that followed the explosions, with parts of the building crumbling, flames everywhere and smoke filling the hallways, the remaining rogues had escaped via the helicopter on the roof.

"So now what?" asked Buzz, after we had watched everything for the second time. "They've wrecked HQ, got us on the run, and gotten rid of our biggest weapon – Alpha Prime."

"Plus, they've still got that transdimensional device," added Smokescreen.

"Well, they've got it, but it's not much use," said Mouse. "It's slaved to an override on my tablet."

He held up his computer tablet. "They need this before they can operate it again."

"Do they know that?" asked Rune.

Mouse shrugged. "If they don't, they will soon enough; the primary screen will be repeating a message that the remote override is in effect. It won't take them long to figure out who's doing it."

"So what's our next move?" I asked between bites of a sandwich - my fifth - that I was eating. (I had been starving after racing through League HQ performing rescues at high speed.)

Buzz turned to Rune. "Any way you can use your magic to get Alpha Prime back?"

"Unlikely," Rune responded. "My magic is powerful enough to cross dimensions, but the simple truth is that I don't know where he is. There are literally billions of places he could be throughout the cosmos. I wouldn't even know where to begin to search."

"I think I can bring Alpha Prime back," Mouse said. "After what happened to Omen and his crew, I made a few small modifications to my own TNIP. Long story short, any pocket dimension it creates now gives off an energy signature that can be tracked. I can free AP, but we need to go back to my lab to do it; there's some equipment there that I need."

"I can teleport you there," I said.

Mouse clapped me on the back. "Thanks."

"I'm in, too," said Smokescreen. "When do we leave?"

"Not you," Mouse told him. "It'll just be me and Kid Sensation. I want you and the rest of the teens who got out to stay here, out of harm's way. And I want the rest of the League members to stay here to protect the injured. Just in case..."

He didn't finish. He didn't have to.

SENSATION

Mouse spent about an hour going on a scavenger hunt around our little hideout. The cameras at HQ had stopped working shortly after the explosions began, so - although he believed everything would be fine - Mouse couldn't swear that his lab equipment would be undamaged. Ergo, he tried to round up anything he might need in order to be prepared.

There wasn't much for me to do but wait. I tried to find Smokey, but after Mouse told him he couldn't accompany us, he'd said a quick adios and disappeared. Finally, Mouse was ready. We said our final goodbyes (again, no Smokey) and then I teleported us to the lab.

SENSATION

Chapter 21

I teleported us inside in insubstantial form. Mouse had stressed that, structurally, he'd designed the lab to withstand almost anything – it even had its own power supply – but it didn't hurt to be safe. (How ironic would it have been to teleport inside just as the ceiling was collapsing?)

Mouse, however, turned out to be right. It was obvious that a number of things had fallen over or been moved out of place due to the explosions, but the lab was essentially intact. The only really noticeable difference was that all of his monitors that were usually streaming a variety of information were dark, resting in some kind of power conservation mode. (According to Mouse, the lab had power, but almost everything - monitors, cameras, etc. - had been knocked offline and would probably need to be rebooted to function properly.)

Mouse immediately went to work, plugging his tablet into a nearby computer bank. Then he pulled a second tablet - along with several other devices, plugs and wires - from a nearby desk drawer. After connecting several of the devices with some of the other items that he'd brought from the safe house, he put the two tablets side-by-side on a tabletop and then began typing furiously, with one hand on each.

I could tell without asking that he was seriously multi-tasking, so I tried to remain as quiet and unobtrusive as possible. I looked around. The place looked a little odd with all of Mouse's monitors turned off. I leaned against a wall and thought about everything that had happened over the last few days.

SENSATION

After a few minutes, I felt my eyes getting droopy. It shouldn't have been that surprising; I hadn't had any sleep in almost twenty-four hours. I went into Mouse's bathroom, intending to splash some water on my face.

The cold water had a little bite but was also refreshing and perked me up a little. I glanced around the bathroom, not surprised to find that Mouse also had a monitor in here. However, I was caught off guard when, a moment later, the monitor came on.

Instead of data, the monitor showed a picture – a somewhat nondescript room with a girl tied to a chair. The girl was blindfolded, but I already knew who it was. *Electra.* Two of Paramount's thugs – Herc and a guy known as HammerHand – stood on either side of her. They weren't brandishing any weapons, but they didn't have to. They were strong enough to rip someone in half with their bare hands.

A message scrolled across the bottom of the screen:

GO TO THE MAIN CONFERENCE ROOM. TELL NO ONE.

I took a second to think about it. I hadn't even thought about Electra since our angry confrontation earlier. I didn't even notice that she hadn't made it out of the building. The real question now was, was she in on it? Of course the message, which continued to scroll across the screen, presaged a trap, but was she part of it? Fake bait? Not that it mattered. I really didn't have a choice.

I walked out of the bathroom and simply told Mouse that I needed to check on something. He

167

acknowledged me with an almost imperceptible nod of the head, his focus on the two tablets.

I debated possibly giving him a clue mentally or telekinetically, but it was obvious that they were watching me. Therefore, knowing that I couldn't tell him any more, I teleported to the conference room.

****

There was no one there when I popped in. Maybe they had expected me to take the stairs.

There was, however, a laptop on the conference room table. Its screen showed the same scene that I'd been privy to before: Electra flanked by the two guys. I took a seat and waited.

After about two minutes, the door opened and Goon came in, drinking what appeared to be coffee out of a mug. He was wearing a blue jogging suit and tennis shoes.

"Before we get started, let me lay out the ground rules," he said. "Just in case you've got any cute notions of teleporting me somewhere crazy, there's a scanner in here set to my biometrics. If it stops reading me as being present in this room before I give the proper signal, our guys will turn your girlfriend into more pieces than Humpty Dumpty."

He smiled at me smugly. "Do we understand each other?"

"We do," I said flatly.

"Good. Now, you have something we want. The override for the TNIP."

"*I* don't have it."

168

SENSATION

"Of course you don't, genius; that was a figure of speech. The only person who could possibly have it is Mouse. But you're going to get it from him and bring it to us. You do that, and you get little Miss Plug-and-Socket back."

"You guys have all the muscle you could wish for; you could break down the door and overrun Mouse's lab in a second. Why do you need me?"

"Because you can get close to Mouse without him suspecting anything. If we try to bum-rush him, he may destroy the override control. Or worse, someone may get hurt. And truth be told, we really don't want to hurt anybody."

He said this with what he apparently thought was a sincere smile, as if he really expected me to believe him. Of course, there was no way they were going to let us just walk out of here, even if I did do what they were asking.

"So," he said, when I didn't respond. "Do we have a deal?"

"Where's your boss?" I asked, abruptly changing the subject. "The one with the brains. The one who's calling the shots. Paramount."

Goon frowned, not liking that. "He's not my boss. We're all in this together."

"Well, he's certainly the brains of the outfit. Otherwise, why isn't he here?"

Goon snickered. "Oh, he's around."

"No, I mean why isn't he in here with me?"

Frowning now, Goon asked, "What are you trying to say? That he tricked me into coming in here?"

"Well, he knew better than to come himself, scanner or not. Speaking of which, it sounds like you only need to be present to the extent necessary to give off a biometric reading."

While he wrestled for a second with what I was saying, I looked at his coffee mug, mentally bisected it from top to bottom, and then used my teleportation power.

"What–" he started to say, when all of a sudden hot coffee spilled over his shoes. He looked at his coffee mug, suddenly noticing that all he was holding was the handle and half of a cup. It looked like it had been neatly sliced in half with a laser from top to bottom. Looking around, he saw the other half of the mug on the conference table where I'd teleported it, spilling its contents across the tabletop.

I looked at my fingernails nonchalantly, trying to appear as though I did things like this all the time. In fact, it was the first time I'd ever even tried to teleport only a portion of something. "As I was saying, apparently only enough of you needs to stay in here to give off a biometric reading."

Goon looked at me, eyes bulging. He no longer appeared smug. In fact, he looked downright nauseous. (The thought of having half your body – maybe your legs – teleported elsewhere can do that to you.) To his credit, he recovered faster than I anticipated.

"This, uh, this, uh, this doesn't change anything. Do we, uh, do we have a, a deal?"

I looked back at the screen, to the picture of Electra still tied to the chair. This time, instead of looking at her, I focused on the room she was in: the walls, the floor…anything that would give me more detail.

SENSATION

It worked before; why not again? The principle is the same.

"I need an answer," he said. "Do we have a deal?"

"Sure," I said resolutely. "You can expect me to deal harshly with you before this is over."

Then, for the first time in my life, I teleported myself to a place that I had never actually been.

And walked straight into a trap.

SENSATION

Chapter 22

I didn't realize it was a trap initially. I popped into the room where Electra was being held. I saw her, then tried to encase her in my power and teleport out. (Emphasis on *tried*.)

Nothing happened. I tried again, with the same result. It was then that I realized the trap I was in. The room I had teleported myself into was also home to a nullifier. I wasn't in one of the League's formal nullifier cells - it was a makeshift one - but it was just as effective.

At the same time, the two guys flanking Electra realized that someone else was in the room. They turned around, and only hesitated a second before they charged.

The good news is that years of training under the tutelage of BT and Gramps had made me an excellent hand-to-hand combatant. Moreover, I'd also been versed in how to fight multiple adversaries at once. These two were obviously just brawlers who were used to simply applying brute force to every problem – especially fights. But they had never received any formal training (or if they had received any, they hadn't paid attention). Thus, in a nullifier cell, without their super strength, they were seriously outclassed, despite being bigger and stronger.

Herc, who was on my left, was closer and got to me first. I reached out, grabbed him and performed a judo throw, using his own momentum to flip him. He landed hard on the floor, the wind knocked out of him. He may also have had some broken bones. He groaned but didn't move.

The other one, HammerHand, grabbed me from behind in a bear hug. I kicked back as hard as I could and felt my heel connect with his shin. He screamed and let me go, then fell to the floor clutching his leg. I didn't think I'd broken it, but it wasn't for lack of trying.

I didn't waste any time, but hurried to Electra to untie her. That's when I heard a door open, and all of a sudden there were bodies all over me.

It was very much like Feral's fight on the security footage. I punched and hit and tried to apply martial arts techniques, but there were just too many of them. They were destined to win by sheer weight of numbers, and in short order I found a dozen strong hands pinning my arms behind my back.

That's when Paramount came in. He had a look of extreme satisfaction on his face.

"Well, if it isn't the great Kid Sensation," he said.

"I'm glad you didn't say '*late*, great,'" I replied.

He smiled. "A sense of humor. That's good. It shows you haven't lost hope. And the truth of the matter is that there's still hope for you yet."

"What are you talking about?"

"Hope that you might join us. Aqua tried to recruit you when she came to your room. I was surprised that it didn't work. Most guys find her powers of persuasion irresistible."

For the first time, I noticed Aqua leaning against a far wall, with Incendia next to her. They each winked and blew a kiss at me simultaneously. My hypothesis about them having some type of mental connection was starting to look less theoretical and more factual by the second.

"In truth," Paramount continued, "my conversion actually started with you. I should be thanking you, since you're the one who showed me the way."

"What do you mean?"

173

SENSATION

A weird gleam came into his eyes. "Until you made him disappear two years ago, I didn't realize how much I hated him. How much I wanted him dead."

With a jolt like lightning, a sudden realization came upon me as to who he was talking about.

"Alpha Prime? Your father? Why would you hate him?"

Unexpected rage suddenly erupted from him. "You have no idea what it's like to have to be his son! To have to constantly live with the comparison! Always knowing that you'll never be good enough!"

"That's crazy!" I shouted. "Everybody knows that you were being groomed to take over, that you would be the world's premiere superhero one day!"

He laughed maniacally, then leaned in close to me. "You honestly don't have a clue, do you? No one does. Well, let me enlighten you. There was never going to be a day that I would take over, never going to be an opportunity for me to say, 'This is my time.'

"My father came to this world over eighty years ago," he continued. "Do you know what he looked like then? The same way he looks now. Scientists have studied him, and as far as they can tell, he's practically a living god."

"And you're just like him!" I interjected. "You've got his genes!"

"No." He shook his head. "I've only got half his genes. Do you know what that means? According to doctors, I will probably live an extraordinarily long life. And I'm not talking a hundred or two hundred years here. I'm talking thousands....thousands of years."

He put his head down, then went on. "Do you have any idea of what life is like when all you have to look forward to is being a poor man's substitute for something else? When all people see when they look at you is a grainy copy of the original?"

"That's why you got rid of him," I said, understanding.

"What did you expect???!!! He can't be beaten! He can't be killed! He's never going to grow old, and he'll never die! If I were only going to live a normal lifespan, maybe it would be tolerable. But a millennium of living in his shadow? Two? Ten? Living for eons and never having a chance to be my own man? I've barely made it through eighteen years. The thought of that being my life was unbearable."

"So you made a deal with supervillains."

"Yes. At least that way, I get to live my own life, right or wrong. I get to make my own choices. And now, you get to make yours."

That's when I saw what he had in his hand. It was BT's inhibitor collar.

"No!" I screeched, instinctively trying to lean back, away from him. My powers were a part of me. Part of who I was. Losing them would be as agonizing as losing a limb.

I struggled like a wild man, but I was simply held too tightly; there was nowhere to go. He slipped the collar around my neck and I heard it lock in place. He held up a small controller in his hand and pressed a button. At the same time, the inhibitor began making a high, keening noise which soon faded.

"Now, let's make sure we understand each other," Paramount said, looking at me levelly. "This inhibitor is particularly attuned to you. With this controller, which is modified to work for me and only me, I can turn it off or

175

on. And just so you don't get cute, the inhibitor is also equipped with a bomb. In other words, I will dissolve the current partnership between your head and neck if you don't do what I want. So–"

"I already know the spiel," I said. "You want me to bring you Mouse's tablet so you can bring the TNIP back online and free your masters."

"Not exactly," Paramount said, laughing. "I want you to bring me his tablet so I can make sure they *never* get free."

The shock must have shown on my face. It was also reflected on the faces of several members of his little army, including Incendia and Aqua.

"Uh, Paramount," Aqua began, "that wasn't the plan. We're supposed to free the Masters–"

"I don't have any masters!" Paramount screamed.

"What?" he said, looking round at his cohorts. "You think I threw off the yoke of my father just to put on that of another bunch of costumed clowns? Who do you think destabilized their device in the first place?"

This was almost more than I could contemplate, so I could only imagine the shock of his followers, who looked back and forth at each other while processing all this in disbelief. I had seriously underestimated Paramount, in terms of abilities and ambition. So had the League. So had his friends. And so, especially, had his one-time masters – the supervillains now trapped in another dimension.

"So you've been going off-script this entire time? Doing your own thing?" I asked. "Including framing me for murder?"

"Actually, that order came from the Masters," he answered. "*Former* Masters, I should say. Kubosh was a meta with a recently-developed tracking ability, and he was hired to locate you."

That explained why Kubosh hadn't tried to run me to ground before and get the reward. He'd only recently gained the power to track things down. Too bad it wasn't an ability that did him much good in the long run.

Paramount went on. "Once we helped him cross your trail – you can thank Omen and his visions for that – it was just a matter of time before he found you. However, he got greedy, tried to play both ends from the middle. He told us about your little mansion hangout outside of town, but then he tried to collect the reward on Kid Sensation by telling the Alpha League your whereabouts. Omen and his buddies felt that was a little bit of a betrayal, and the rest is history."

"How'd you know about the inhibitor?" I asked.

"Omen again. In one of his visions of the future, he saw how it could be used to take away your powers. Which brings us back to the current plan," he said. "The nullifier is now off. In a minute, I'm going to turn the inhibitor off, and you..."

His voice trailed off as I stopped paying attention to what he was saying.

The nullifier is off???!!! Didn't he know that the inhibitor was only partially effective at the best of times?

I didn't wait to hear the end of his speech. I switched into super speed and then ran forward to snatch the controller from his hand. Then I wrapped my mind around Electra and attempted to teleport...

And found myself in Mouse's lab, along with a still-bound Electra. I could only imagine Paramount's face as we disappeared, but we didn't have time to gloat.

Goon had met me in the conference room right here at HQ. I had a funny feeling that Paramount's entire crew was fairly close.

"Mouse!" I screamed. "I've got an inhibitor collar with a bomb!"

Mouse stopped what he was doing and ran over.

"Here," I said, handing him the controller. "This is what's supposed to detonate it."

The inhibitor was making that keening noise again. I felt for sure the bomb was about to go off, and then the noise began to die down like it did before.

"Hurry!" I shouted. "Before this thing explodes!"

Mouse raced over to a nearby workbench and grabbed some kind of toolkit. In less than ten seconds he had the controller case open and was fiddling with wires. I gave him the seriously condensed version of what had happened, taking less than thirty seconds to do so.

By the time I finished, Mouse looked up and said, "Okay, you should be good for now. If it goes off, it won't be from this." He tapped the controller.

"Hey," Mouse shouted at someone behind me. "Untie Electra from that chair."

For the first time, I noticed that there were other people in the room. Basically, about a dozen teens were milling around, seemingly doing odd jobs around the lab: moving boxes, sorting equipment, and so on.

"Who are they?" I asked Mouse, who was now examining the inhibitor with some odd-looking instruments.

"Ask your friend," Mouse answered. I looked around and saw Smokescreen, grinning as he walked towards me.

"I know what Mouse said about playing it safe," Smokey said, "but I couldn't let you guys try to make this stand alone. So I rounded up what members of the teen supers I could and came as fast as possible."

"And almost got shot for his trouble," Mouse inserted. "They showed up right after you left. I thought it was Paramount and his guys trying to get in and almost blasted them. He's lucky I don't have an itchy trigger finger."

Nobody said anything else as Mouse continued examining the inhibitor collar. I tried to look around and noticed Electra being helped to her feet. She rubbed her wrists in an obvious effort to get circulation going again after being tied up for an extended period. She saw me looking and mouthed "Thank you." I just nodded in response, but I noticed that she began to make her way towards us.

"Okay," Mouse finally said. "Good news and bad news."

"Great," I muttered. "Another mixed report."

"I'll take that as you wanting the good news first," Mouse retorted. "Basically, you should still have most of your powers, and the bomb isn't likely to go off."

"'Most' of my powers?" I said incredulously. "What exactly does that mean?"

"Well, that's tied into the bad news. From what I can see, this inhibitor has some type of adaptive logic circuit. Basically, as you use your powers it learns about them and then figures out how to block them. Afterwards, as long as you have it on, you won't have that ability anymore."

"Are you sure?" Electra asked. "Because he just teleported us here."

179

Mouse made a vague gesture. "Go ahead and try it."

I attempted to teleport to the other side of the room. Nothing. Likewise when I tried to shift into super speed. Almost embarrassingly, I told Mouse that he appeared to be right.

"Unfortunately, there's more," he said. "It's locked into your biometrics."

"What does that mean?" I asked.

"It means that, for all intents and purposes, that collar is now like an additional limb or appendage. Where you go, it goes. Didn't you notice that you teleported here with it still on?"

In all honesty, I hadn't even thought about trying to teleport without it; at the time, I was just trying to get away, and I admitted as much.

"Normally that would be a foolish oversight," Mouse said, "but in this case it wouldn't have mattered. Like I said, it's locked in to your biometrics. If you teleport, it teleports; if you phase, it phases. You're stuck with it for now."

The shock and desolation must have shown on my face, because Mouse laid a reassuring hand on my shoulder.

"Buck up, Kid," he said. "We'll fix this, assuming we have time."

Just then, there came a booming, thunderous pounding on the door to Mouse's lab, followed by the tortured screech of tearing metal.

Paramount and his crew were coming in.

SENSATION

Chapter 23

"Move!" Mouse shouted, grabbing his computer tablets and rushing to the floor-to-ceiling bookcase on the side of the lab. "Follow me!"

I missed seeing what he did, but the bookshelf quickly slid right, into a recessed area set in the wall. Standing where the bookshelf had been a second ago was a monstrous, vault-like door. As it began to slowly open, I could hear the hiss of hydraulics.

Everyone began hustling inside as soon as the vault door was wide enough to permit ingress. Mouse went first, and I saw a light come on somewhere inside. All of the other teens began scrambling in, followed by Electra and Smokey. I was last.

As I slipped inside, the bookcase shot out from its hidden area, once again covering the vault door. Presumably Mouse had a remote for the thing, because I hadn't done anything to put it back into place. He must also have had one for the vault door, because it stopped opening and slowly reversed course, preparing to close.

Looking around, I noticed that we were in a cavernous chamber. There were a few chairs and tables – including one where Mouse currently sat on the far side of the room – but the most overriding feature of the room were the containers. Everywhere you looked there were boxes and crates and bins. There were even long rows of shelves that appeared to hold various bric-a-brac and miscellaneous objects. This was clearly a storage room of some type.

Through the bookcase, I heard the door to Mouse's lab finally yielding and the rhythmic thudding of heavy feet running into the room.

SENSATION

"Find them!" I heard Paramount snarl. "They're here somewhere."

There was an odd cadence established by feet running willy-nilly all over the place, as well as the sound of equipment being knocked over.

Suddenly, the vault's hydraulics made a clear, squeaking noise. It was followed by an "Over here!" from somewhere nearby in the lab. I found myself trying to will the door to go faster. I even pressed my back against it and pushed, as well as used my telekinesis to try to get it closed.

That was a near-fatal error. My telekinesis helped for a few seconds, and then the inhibitor began keening once more. Suddenly it stopped. I tried using my telekinesis again, but to no avail, it was gone.

Right about then, I heard the bookshelf being ripped away, torn up from its moorings. And just as the vault was about to close, a big, meaty paw thrust its way through, trying to keep the door wedged open.

I didn't recognize the arm, which was through the opening to about mid-bicep, but whoever owned it obviously had super strength. The door had stopped closing, and the hydraulics were actually making painful noises as they attempted to seal the vault.

"Move your arm!" I screamed.

"Make me!" shouted the arm's owner, someone I didn't recognize.

Smokey and Electra raced over and added their weight to mine in an attempt to close the door. Still, even with all three of us pushing, we were losing the battle.

Deciding on a bold move, I made the arm insubstantial. The inhibitor again started with the noise, while the vault door – now with no physical impediments

– actually started to close again, passing through the phased arm. After what seemed like an eternity but was actually just a few seconds, the vault door closed and locked itself – with the insubstantial arm still sticking through it.

"Move your arm!" I screamed again. "If you want to keep this arm you need to move it now!"

The response was what I assumed to be a blow from his other hand, so powerful that it made the metal of the vault door bulge. The arm swung deliriously to and fro, with the hand opening and closing almost spasmodically in an attempt to find purchase on something. Obviously the owner of the arm didn't realize what had happened - that his arm was now insubstantial - and was trying to find anything on our side of the vault to grab or grip.

Suddenly, the noise from the inhibitor stopped. There was a bloodcurdling scream of pain and anguish from the other side of the vault, and the arm that had been phased a second ago fell to the ground, solid and twitching and bloody.

Electra covered her mouth and gasped in horror. Smokey looked like he was going to be sick.

"Mouse," I said, kicking the dismembered arm away, "how's it coming?"

"I need more time," was his only response. His fingers were flying across the surfaces of the two tablets.

The sound of painful screaming on the other side of the vault continued but decreased in volume, as if the person had moved away from the door. And all of a sudden there was more insistent pounding on the vault. In particular, the bulge that had been created in the door earlier was getting bigger, as if someone had designated it an obvious weak point and began exploiting it.

I kept my weight on the door, but it wouldn't be any use for much longer. Moreover, water had begun seeping in under the bottom of the door and around the frame. *Aqua, trying to get in.*

"Move!" shouted Electra.

I stepped away, and she shot a bolt of electricity into the water on the floor. There was a painful yelp that seemed to come from several places at once, and the water withdrew almost too fast to see. However, the pounding continued, and the bulge was extending well into our side of the room. Moreover, the frame that the vault sat in was starting to bend and warp as the strength of those on the other side began to prove superior to the metal of the door and its housing.

I threw myself against the door again, determined to buy Mouse every second I could. Electra and Smokey joined me, but I wasn't sure it would do much good. Truthfully, we just needed more weight. Then I had a thought about where I could possibly get some.

Earlier, I had been asked about using my phasing power to increase my density. Again, it was something I'd never done before, but the principle wasn't really very different from phasing. In fact, it was pretty much the same as when I returned a phased object to its original solid form. However, instead of just leaving an object as I found it, this time I wanted to keep going, making the object a bit more solid – denser, heavier. And in this case, the object was me.

It was an odd sensation. First, I reached out with my mind, the way I would have if I were trying to phase myself. But rather than become insubstantial, I focused on doing the exact opposite – becoming *more* substantial, so to speak. I imagined my entire body - my bones, muscle, tissue, sinew - all becoming more packed...more condensed...thicker...heavier...

I wasn't sure it was working, but then I heard the whine of the inhibitor. That meant I was doing something – hopefully what I intended.

At the same time, there was a mighty smack against the weakened vault door that echoed throughout the area - like a hammer ringing out against steel - and the bulge ripped open with a metallic shriek. Through the gap it now provided came a powerful-looking, well-muscled arm. The door was yielding fast.

The hand at the end of the arm reached around madly, obviously trying to find what, if anything, was helping wedge the door shut. Electra and Smokey scrambled out of the way, but I stayed put, still trying to keep weight on the door. I leaned away from the hand as far as I felt I could without compromising my position on the vault.

I looked to see how Mouse was doing. There was a glowing sphere next to him now, and inside it a vague but recognizable figure: Alpha Prime. Mouse had found him, but needed more time to dissolve the dimensional pocket.

With greater speed and agility than I imagined, the hand through the door suddenly latched onto my shoulder. Then it began to squeeze.

"Open the door!" a voice on the other side demanded, as the hand squeezed harder.

The inhibitor was giving off a high-pitched squeak now. Its logic circuit seemed to be having trouble getting a lock on what I was doing – probably due to the fact this was a power (or an aspect of a power) that I really hadn't tried before.

The hand continued its unrelenting assault on my shoulder, and I screamed as I felt bones starting to grind painfully against each other in unnatural fashion. Smokey yelled at Electra to fry the arm with her electricity.

"I can't!" Electra answered. "I'll electrocute Jim, too!"

Instead, both she and Smokey beat at the hand and arm ineffectually with their fists. I don't think the person on the other side even noticed. As for me, I was pouring everything I had into a two-fold mission: continuing to increase my body's overall density, and – in particular – making my trapped shoulder as dense and solid as possible.

The inhibitor, still unable to get a lock on my power, kept up its insidious whining. Under my feet, I felt the floor beginning to buckle and crumble as my massively increased density and weight put unwarranted pressure on it. The pain in my shoulder slowly lessened as my body became firmer, harder. I could feel my assailant growing frustrated and trying to squeeze harder as the former suppleness of my shoulder gave way to something more compact.

Suddenly, the whining of the inhibitor came to a halt. The hand continued trying to cause damage, but it was just a bit of a nuisance now. Looking around, I saw that almost all eyes in the room were fixated on me. The only exception was Mouse, who worked unceasingly to try to free his teammate. On his part, Alpha Prime was clearly visible, and I could actually hear him trying to say something. It seemed to be directed at me, but the sound came through muffled and distorted, making it impossible to figure out what he was trying to convey.

"Step aside," demanded a disturbingly calm voice on the other side of the door. It was Paramount, and at his order the hand and arm withdrew. The sound of his voice gave me an odd chill, and it dawned on me with clear certainty what he was about to do.

"Get back!" I screamed at those near me, wildly gesticulating. I don't think anyone realized what was about to happen, but an eerie blue light began to seep in around the frame of the door and the hole where the hand had come through.

"Kid, cover that door!" boomed a loud voice. It was Alpha Prime, not yet free but finally coherent.

In fact, I had already begun shapeshifting as soon as I realized what was happening, not taking on any particular form but rather just trying to stretch myself high enough and wide enough to blanket the vault door in its entirety. The inhibitor was making noise again but I ignored it, focusing instead on any place where the azure color was seeping in and trying to cover it. The blue light was an indicator of the areas I needed to block, but also confirmed my worst fears.

Paramount was preparing to fire his Bolt Blast. His most powerful weapon. The one that could obliterate anything.

I looked around the room one last time. I saw a bunch of teens, terrified for the most part and attempting to hide behind boxes and bins. With Paramount so unhinged, it was unlikely that many on our side would survive this day – me among them. But I could buy them – buy Mouse – a few more precious moments to hope. I could see Alpha Prime punching wildly against the sphere that held him while Mouse continued working feverishly without pause.

I was braced against the door, still trying to stretch my body out, when the inhibitor stopped making noise. That was it; I'd covered as much of the door as I could. Sadly, a few slivers of blue luminescence were still coming through when the light suddenly intensified. I closed my eyes, thinking about all the things I'd done, and all the things I'd never do. How sixteen years just didn't seem like enough time to live a life. How I'd never even had a real girlfriend. How I'd never learned to drive.

Later, I would try to remember exactly what occurred next, but so much seemed to happen almost simultaneously. The door of the vault seemed to bulge out in my direction for a second, and then just melt away. It vanished, like dew evaporating in the morning sun. A cascade of warmth bathed my back, pressed against it like a gentle, soothing massage. Briefly I wondered if this was the afterlife – whether eternity was simply going to feel like faint, ever-expanding warmth.

"No," a voice, Paramount's, uttered in disbelief. "It's impossible!"

I opened my eyes, surprised that I still had eyes to open. I immediately looked behind me, to Mouse's lab. As I did so, something slid off my neck and to the ground. It was the inhibitor. The back of it had been obliterated by Paramount's Bolt Blast; with nothing to hold it in place around my neck, it had simply fallen off.

Paramount was standing about twenty feet away from me, mouth practically agape. All of his henchmen were behind him.

As I suspected, the vault door was nowhere to be found. It had essentially been vaporized. The real question, though, was why hadn't I been expunged along with it?

That apparently was the thing that was also plaguing Paramount, because he suddenly began firing more Bolt Blasts at me.

"Impossible!" he screamed, while continuing to fire at me. "Impossible! Impossible!"

I almost went insubstantial, but then I remembered everyone in Mouse's secret room and stood my ground. The Bolt Blasts hit me, but had no effect.

Oddly enough, it was Paramount's unbridled rage that bought us more time. As long as he was firing Bolt Blasts at me, no one who was with him could rush us. I think this must have occurred to someone else, because several of the people with Paramount tried calling his name, but he didn't seem to hear them. Finally, one of the guys behind him – a red-skinned monstrosity with horns and a forked tail called Daemon - placed a hand on Paramount's shoulder to get his attention.

Paramount angrily turned his gaze on him…and Daemon evaporated from the torso up. There was stunned disbelief for a second, and then his entire group began scattering like chickens trapped in a henhouse with a fox.

Aqua turned to liquid, a puddle on the floor, and then fled underneath some nearby equipment with frightening speed. Incendia became living flame and went streaking out the doorway. One by one, they all scrambled to flee or take cover from their mad leader.

As for Paramount himself, he initially didn't seem to realize what he'd done. After a few seconds it must have sunk in, because the glow of his Bolt Blast faded from his eyes, but by that time most of his followers had fled or were hiding as best they could in Mouse's lab.

His vision swung back to me. "You! This is all your fault!"

He made as if to charge me, but he hadn't taken more than two steps when something flew out of Mouse's hidden room in a blur of speed.

A hand of incalculable strength gripped Paramount's neck in a vise and lifted him off the ground.

Paramount struggled maniacally, beating at the hand that held him in vain. His legs kicked wildly in the air. He looked comically like a child struggling to get away while being held aloft by a parent. In fact, that's exactly what the situation was.

Alpha Prime held his wayward offspring up off the ground by one hand. He turned to look at me.

"Kid, are you okay?" he asked.

"I'm fine," I replied.

"Good, check on the others," he said almost casually, essentially ignoring the struggling giant in his hand. Paramount, on his part, never stopped fighting, and even fired his Bolt Blast at his father. They had no more effect on Alpha Prime than they'd had on me. Alpha Prime sighed and placed his free hand over his son's eyes. Screaming in frustration, Paramount brought both his hands up and tried futilely to pull away the fingers covering his eyes. Not a single digit moved.

Seeing that, I kind of understood now what had caused Paramount such anguish that he became unhinged. Alpha Prime was raw power – limitless, timeless, and absolute. Juxtaposing any human, even a superhuman, against the standard he represented was not just unfair but cruel.

SENSATION

Chapter 24

The next few days were extremely hectic. As it turned out, we didn't escape Paramount's last assault completely unscathed. One poor kid just happened to be in the wrong place at the wrong time and one of Paramount's Bolt Blasts had taken the top of his head off. Another had lost a foot. All in all, however, we were quite lucky.

The security footage had essentially identified everyone who was working with Paramount. However, after eventually being rounded up, quite a few of them claimed to have been intimidated into doing his bidding. Others claimed to have been misled, asserting that Paramount – through his position of leadership – had convinced them that what they were doing was right. Finally, a few hid behind their status as minors under the law, claiming they couldn't be prosecuted. No one knew exactly how it would all shake out.

As for Paramount himself, he was currently being housed at a secure facility in an undisclosed location. I probably could have gotten more details if I wanted to, but I didn't press. Instead, I spent my time essentially being an errand boy for Mouse: go here; go there; do this; do that.

Much to my surprise, it seemed that Mouse was actually the de facto head of Alpha League instead of Alpha Prime, as everyone generally assumed. When I asked him how that had come about, Mouse had just shrugged, making a vague comment about superheroes needing more than just tangible super powers. Other than that, he essentially avoided answering my questions about almost everything, preferring to say that we'd have time to talk later.

Alpha Prime generally kept to himself during this time. Other than helping out with repairs to League HQ, no one really saw him.

"He's got some issues to work out," Rune said when I asked him. "It's not every day that you find out your child is a maniac who wants you dead."

With the threat of imminent harm removed, Braintrust had moved Mom and Gramps to the penthouse suite of a five-star hotel. Needless to say, they were loving it.

I had dinner with them every day. So it was that a few days later when I stopped by for my daily visit I got the surprise of my life.

I'd taken to arriving at their suite in a normal fashion: taking the elevator up, knocking on the door, etc. On this particular occasion, my grandfather opened the door and let me in. Usually, he'd give me a mental hello, but I got nothing this time so I knew that something was going on.

As I followed him into the suite, I heard voices. I recognized my mother's, and the other was also familiar, but a little distorted by the acoustics in the penthouse. I had assumed it was one of BT's clones, but when I entered the living area I saw that I was wrong. Dead wrong.

There he was, sitting on a sofa across from my mother, who was lounging in a recliner. He was wearing a business suit rather than a costume, but I didn't have any trouble recognizing him. I'd studied him my whole life, from every angle, every side, every direction, every perspective. I'd have known him anywhere – in or out of a costume, with or without a cape, in a business suit, in swimming trunks, even in a Santa Claus suit.

It struck me as odd that I knew so much about a man who knew so little about me.

A man who probably couldn't pick me out of a lineup.

A man who probably hadn't thought about me since the day I was born.

Alpha Prime. My father.

That he was here meant only one thing: he knew who I was. My mind was reeling. He'd avoided me my entire life. I really didn't want to deal with this now.

Still staring at him, I took a few steps backwards, then did a full one-eighty and prepared to walk back out the door. My mother's voice brought me up short.

"John Indigo Morrison Carrow!" she screamed, coming to her feet. "Get your butt back over here!"

I rarely heard anyone say my whole name. However, it was a name meant to embody my entire heritage. John was my grandfather's given name, while Indigo was my grandmother. Carrow was our family name, and as for Morrison...well, that was Alpha Prime's actual surname, although few people knew it. For as long as I could remember, though, everyone had always called me "Jim," based on my first three initials. Calling out my full name meant only one thing: Mom was irritated with me. (Not to mention the fact that her eyes, I could sense, were flashing crimson.)

Slowly I turned around and came back into the living room. I kept my eyes downcast.

"Don't be rude, Jim," my mother continued. "We have a guest."

Alpha Prime stood up. "It's okay, Geneva. We've actually already met."

The words sounded odd, out of place - more suited to business acquaintances bumping into each other at a country club rather than father and son. When I still didn't say anything, my mother turned to me.

<Jim, what's the matter with you???!!!> My mother rarely ever used her powers. She was obviously trying to make a point.

<What's he doing here?>

<He's here to see you.>

<Really? Did he say anything about the last sixteen years when he *didn't* want to see me?>

<Stop that! If you stay with those teen supers, you're going to be seeing him every day, so you need to work it out.>

<I was doing fine. Why'd you have to call him?>

<I didn't call him. *He* called *me*.>

That last one was a bit of a shock. I had just assumed that it was my mother who had reached out. Taking my silence for acquiescence, she turned and started leaving the room.

"I'll leave you boys to catch up," she said as she went into her bedroom suite. I looked around for my grandfather, hoping to find support in that corner, but he had conveniently disappeared at some point after letting me in.

With a disgusted sigh, I flopped down and took my mother's spot sitting across from my father. I wasn't ready for this. I hadn't wanted to have this conversation yet. It was one thing to be around him when he didn't have a clue who I was. There was no pressure then, no expectations, no agenda. It was something else when he knew that I was his son, that there was some kind of connection between us.

There was an uncomfortable silence as we both struggled for something to say. Or rather he did; there was no way I was speaking up first. I crossed my arms, sat back and waited.

"Uh, Jim," he began after a few moments, "I just want to say that I'm proud of how you handled yourself during this crisis that we had. I mean, with your...with the situation with Paramount."

"What's going to happen to him?" I asked.

"He's got to face justice for what he's done. But at the same time, it's clear that he also needs therapeutic help. I should have seen what was happening to him."

"Maybe it's a good thing, then, that you weren't around, if that happened right under your nose. Who knows what kind of trouble I might have gotten into?"

He just stared at me for a second. I could tell that I had hit him hard – and possibly below the belt.

"Okay, I probably deserved that," he said after a moment. "But there's no way you'd ever have turned out like that. Not with your mother and grandfather raising you."

"Is that why you weren't around, then? Because you knew that there was somebody else to pick up the slack?"

"I wasn't around because I was already raising Paramount in the middle of a three-ring circus. From the moment he was born, everything he did was news. Cameras were around him night and day. It was an unhealthy environment, and as you can see, it took its toll. By the time you came along two years later, I knew I had to put some distance between us if you ever stood a chance of having a normal childhood."

"Yeah, right. You're father of the year."

"Ask your mother if you don't believe me. She grew up in that same spotlight – the child of two superheroes – and it was no fun. Your grandparents did their best to shield her, but it was still no picnic."

"You talk about my mother like you actually cared about her."

"I did. I do. She came along at a time when I was...lost. Paramount's mother had taken off, I was raising a kid all alone while trying to save the world - *literally* save the world - at the same time. And I was incredibly lonely."

He chuckled. "I know, I know. How can you be lonely when everyone in the world is clamoring to be your friend, to hang out with you, to just be seen with you? And yet, I was. I was a hair's breadth from chucking it all away when your mother came into my life. She saved me."

"Is that why you're here now? Are you lost and needing to be saved again since your number-one son went off the reservation? What was it that made you finally crawl out of the woodwork?"

"The talk we had the other night. Up on the roof."

Now it was my turn to be shell-shocked.

"You...you already knew who I was?"

"Not initially. But right before you disappeared, I apologized to you for that fight we had two years ago, and I saw a flash of color in your eyes. Literal color. Just like your mother and grandmother. I knew who you were then."

"Great, betrayed by my genes." I reflected for a second on that particular legacy of my alien grandmother that my mother and I had both inherited, the physical trait of having our eyes flash color with strong emotions. I can usually keep mine under control, but now I remembered how my eyes had felt irritated when I'd left the roof. I hadn't even considered that it might have been that specific characteristic of my physiognomy.

"I came by your room a few minutes later to talk to you," he continued, "but you never answered the door."

"I wasn't there," I said. "I was next door, talking to Smokescreen."

"Good," he said with a slight smile. "I was afraid that maybe you were avoiding me. Then, a few minutes later, Paramount asked me to meet him in Mouse's lab."

"Where he trapped you." I was already familiar with this part of the story.

"Yes. But the worst part of that whole thing wasn't being trapped. It was thinking that I'd missed a golden opportunity to get to know you - especially when it seemed like I'd just found you again."

"All thanks to my genetically freakish eyes."

"Don't discount the value of your genes. They actually saved your life a few days ago."

"What do you mean?"

"Do you remember when Paramount used his Bolt Blasts on you? How they didn't have an effect?"

"Yeah. I was expecting to die then."

"Well, it's kind of the way that a scorpion's venom won't work on another scorpion. In this particular case, the Bolt Blast doesn't work on family members."

Something suddenly occurred to me. "That's why you shouted for me to cover the door when we were in the vault. You knew his blasts wouldn't hurt me."

"Yes, *I* knew, but *you* didn't. You didn't know, but you did it anyway, even if it meant you'd die."

"I wasn't thinking about that. I just knew that people were depending on me."

"And it's that type of selflessness that makes someone valuable, regardless of whether they have powers or not." He suddenly stood up. "Look, I know it's not going to happen overnight, but I'd like it if we could start working on having some kind of relationship."

He extended his hand. I stared at it for a moment, then took it. He smiled.

****

A few days later, Mouse asked me to come by his lab to talk. It was probably the first part of HQ that they completed repairs on – no doubt at Mouse's insistence. (Rank has its privileges.) When I showed up, he didn't waste any time on small talk.

"When we had our talk before - after your confrontation on the football field with Paramount - you tried to warn me about him. You knew he was a bad seed, didn't you?"

I just shrugged and stared off into space.

"How did you know?" he asked.

I sighed. "I'm an empath, and I've also been working as a bounty hunter. I've discovered that some of the bad ones give off a certain type of emotional vibe. There's a certain callousness in their personality, a disregard or disrespect for some aspects of common decency."

"And you picked up on that from Paramount."

"I felt something along those lines, but…" I stared off to the side, unsure of how much to say.

"But what?"

I let out a long breath and looked Mouse in the eye. "He was a jerk and a bully. He's not someone I would have ever called a friend or hung out with. But I just couldn't believe he was *all* bad, because…"

I took another deep breath. "Because he's my brother. Alpha Prime…" I trailed off, unable to finish.

He didn't speak for a moment, then simply said, "I see."

****

I left Mouse's lab feeling wretched about my entire existence. A long-lost father who finally put in an appearance. An evil half-brother who probably wants me dead. My life was nothing but a horrid bundle of overworked clichés. I was so lost in my own world, that I didn't even notice Electra until she was almost on top of me.

I had seen her in passing over the past few days, but we hadn't really had a chance to talk. Instead, on those few occasions when we were actually in close proximity, we had simply gone through the motions of exchanging perfunctory pleasantries and then gone our separate ways.

This encounter appeared to be going along the same lines, although extended by us engaging in some additional meaningless chitchat about the weather and whatnot. After that concluded, we both just kind of stood there, each essentially waiting on the other to say something material or worthwhile. When it appeared that that wasn't going to happen, I took the next logical step.

"So," I said, slowly meandering away, "I guess I'll see you around."

"Yeah," she said unenthusiastically. "See ya."

I'd taken maybe five steps when I heard her call out to me.

"Hey," she said, closing the distance between us as I turned around, "a couple of us are going to that Super-Egos concert this weekend. I've got an extra ticket if you want to come."

I smiled. "Why, Electra, are you asking me on a date?"

"No," she said, giving me a playful punch on the shoulder. "I'm just trying to apologize for what happened last time... for shocking you and locking you in a nullifier cell."

"And...?"

She rolled her eyes. "And to thank you for rescuing me when I was tied up."

"In that case, I'd love to come."

"Great!" she said, then added with a wink and a smile, "It's a date."

I grinned, suddenly gleeful at this happy turn of events. Sure, my life wasn't perfect, and maybe it was riddled with clichés, but I had a funny feeling that with a little effort, I might really enjoy it.